The Last Sandcastle

for Anne

The O'Brien Press Fiction Editor:
Peter Fallon

The Last Sandcastle

JEREMY LELAND

THE O'BRIEN PRESS

DUBLIN

PUBLISHED 1983 BY THE O'BRIEN PRESS
20 VICTORIA ROAD, DUBLIN 6, IRELAND

COPYRIGHT JEREMY LELAND

British Library Cataloguing in Publication Data
Leland, Jeremy
The Last Sandcastle
I. Title
B23'.914 [F]   PR6062.E/
ISBN 0-86278-051-9 hardback
ISBN 0-86278-052-7 paperback

ACKNOWLEDGEMENTS ARE DUE TO THE EDITORS OF
NEW IRISH WRITING (THE IRISH PRESS), AND THE
FICTION NETWORK, SAN FRANCISCO.

PUBLISHED WITH THE ASSISTANCE OF THE ARTS COUNCIL/
AN CHOMHAIRLE EALAÍON, IRELAND
BOOK DESIGN: MICHAEL O'BRIEN
TYPESETTING: REDSETTER LTD.
PRINTED BY CAHILL PRINTERS LTD. DUBLIN
COVER PRINTED BY COLERIDGE LTD. DUBLIN

Contents

The Lake

The lake was like a silver plain. Small eyes opening and shutting were
the nearest there was to waves on its vast surface. Except for the
swirls Eilís made with her oars. She had rowed with an angry determination. Now she was nearly a mile from the shore, she rested,
calmer. The boat was old, of a heavy build, its gunwhale scarred
from usage, its thwarts worn and bleached from forty years of cor-
duroy and denim, mostly her uncle's bony bottom. He allowed her
to take the boat out when he didn't need it for fishing.

The sky above was an immense impacted greyness. It seemed
unlikely that the gulls and crows could fly across it unimpeded. The
water slapped quietly at the hull, the oars dripped. She loved the
isolation of the lake before the tourist season, when cabin cruisers
appeared like tents pitched all over a field. She took every opportun-
ity to come out upon its surface, though it was not often so benign
at this time of the year. Six foot waves were not uncommon. It was
after all, some twenty miles in length.

She watched three mallards fly over in their straight accurate
manner, two drakes lusting after a duck. On the post of a navigation
marker she could see a cormorant standing, black and priestlike.
Near the tip of a small island a pair of coots were swimming in and
out of the rocks, heads nodding. The water below her was dark,
slightly flecked like the iris of an eye, with tiny pieces of bog. All her
anger had gone, erased as if it had never existed.

During the week she worked in a shop. It was pillared with Victorian slender iron poles with lotus capitals which held up a tracery
of light iron trusses and herringbone patterns of white-painted
timber. But this unmodernised interior was obscured by the impact
of a display of placards, manufacturers' advertisements for the covering of significant parts of female anatomy. Wherever one looked
there were voluptuous bosoms encased in embroidered brassières
and bottoms streamlined in lacework pants. And everywhere,
shelves of packets and glass-fronted cabinets crammed with an

incredible variety of these garments. Of course, there were also racks of dresses, tailored trousers, blouses, skirts and, in the windows, willowy plastic models simpered in black nightdresses and crimson ball-gowns.

She despised the work, especially when called into one of the small changing cubicles and confronted with other women's obsession with the appearance of their breasts, being drawn into hypochondriacal discussions. And yet, she was held there by the minor significance she had, in others' need for her advice. In that emporium she was the expert. There were so many insecure women. Sometimes they even whispered about breast cancer. Could she tell?

She dipped the oars back into the quiet water, pulled the boat on in the manner peculiar to rowers who travel backwards by leaning forwards, uncertain of where they are going, but seeing all that they are leaving. Why did she stay? She kept insisting to herself that she should leave, leave the town, leave the area, go and find herself an occupation that used her mind. She had no friends, no commitments. She was solitary by inclination, preferring the sardonic chatter of her own mind to the frivolous prattle of others.

She liked her uncle. He was small and taciturn, his conversation mostly single words delivered like shutting a door, as if he resented talking. He had only two interests in life, fishing and cattle. Those two subjects would fire him occasionally to whole sentences. She did not live with him, although he was her only living relative. No woman could have lived in his house. All he needed to do was put a sign outside, and people entering would have thought it a junk shop, and seen no evidence whatever that anyone lived there. She had a flat in the town above a dentist's surgery.

The other person she liked was Mrs. O'Murphy, who owned the shop. She was a tall woman with hair like pastry pressed over her cranium and the crust spreading sideways in a frill. Her husband, not long dead from drink, had been English, and changed his name to the phony-sounding one he had left her with, thinking it would help the business, blend in with the locals. He had become a Catholic and left her with five children. She liked to sing, wherever she went, whatever she was doing, as unselfconsciously as other people light up cigarettes. Her voice was light, though rather indistinct, as if she were never certain of the words; the songs were mostly traditional. It was a habit no one thought the least odd, or questioned, or even really noticed, since she'd done it ever since anyone could remember. With the problems of running the shop and coping with five children on her own, Eilís concluded her singing kept her sane.

She pulled past Barge Island, so named because a Guinness barge had been wrecked on it long ago, and its rocks had become piled with broached casks, and the air around it had stunk of sour stout for years, like a rotting corpse.

A woman had come into the shop that morning, insisted she was size twelve, and since the customer is always right, had to be indulged, though anyone could see she was at least a sixteen. Within five minutes she had burst the bodice of a sixty pound dress, complained that modern stitching was atrocious, and stalked coolly out of the shop. Eilís caught up with her on the pavement, demanded payment. The woman refused.

—You can't play the ugly sister and get away with it, said Eilís. The woman had gone red, become incoherent with fury, pushed her into the road and hurried away. The incident had rankled all day, it had an ugliness she could not get out of her head. It was her own failure to handle it that galled her. It spoiled her independence. It was this anger that had made her row far out into the lake.

A heron flapped with slow wingbeat round the far side of the trees on the island. Very private birds, she thought. One usually only saw them leaving discreetly, they always seemed to contrive to fly the far side of any obstacles. Only when intent on their fishing, turned to a stick in the water, did they sometimes neglect their caution. She had come in a half-circle within a mile of the southern shore. She had come further than she thought. Towards the west the thick grey dome of the sky had split along its edge with thin creamy openings.

Dusk would fall within the hour. She turned back, heading across a stretch of open water of about a mile towards the church island just off shore from her uncle's spit of land.

—I often wonder why you stay here, Eilís, Margaret O'Murphy had said to her, while they were checking a newly-arrived consignment of lingerie.

—You're a great asset to me, you give the place a touch of class, I know you'll say your uncle's only a farmer, but you have a look of being foreign, people keep saying to me, is she French or something, all right, so they don't know you get your complexion from going out on the lake in all weathers, and you get your ways from doing a BA in Dublin, but there's more to it than that, I know you'll never tell me what goes on inside your head, and I like you for it, you know I'm fond of you, I don't mind if others say you're toffee-nosed, you never join in anything, ignore them, you're the cat that walks by itself, but I feel you're unhappy, I often wonder how it is you never have a man, sorry, I know that's getting personal, your life's your own, but it's not as if you're not good-looking, you dress a treat, even in your oldest clothes you manage to look good, how is it you can do that, and yet give the brush-off to every Tom, Dick and Harry within a hundred miles. I'd love to know what goes on inside that head of yours, maybe you'll tell us one day what it is you want out of this world, but I feel you're not happy here, aren't I right?

Turning her head to check her direction, Eilís noticed what she thought at first was a rock just showing above the waterline, where no rock should be, this was supposed to be deep open water. Pausing to study it, she came to the conclusion it was something floating, and out of curiosity changed direction to pass closer. The rowlocks creaked rhythmically. The sounds of birds on the distant shores carried across the still water, moorhens and curlews. Far across on the west side of the lake, in what might be called the shipping lane, there was the muffled burble of a cabin-cruiser's engine.

She turned to look again, and held her breath. The conformation of the floating object rang in her mind with signal clarity. To one human-being, even the faintest suggestion of another, is instantly recognisable. Her first instinct was to turn tail, row away from it as fast as possible. But slowly she came closer, edging the boat till she was alongside the waterlogged jeans and t-shirt that confined the figure of a drowned man.

He was on his back, torso, knees, bare feet and left hand just awash, right hand hung down, head tilted back. Her first reaction of horror gave way to one of pity. She pulled the oars in, leaned over the edge and pulled him past by his belt-buckle, then kneeling on the thwart slipped an arm deep into the water to raise his head. He was young, black-haired, with bony handsome features. His eyes were closed, long lashes matted over his wet cheeks. She thought that in all her life she had never looked upon such a good-looking man.

Suddenly she was galvanised into action. She must pull him aboard. Perhaps she could empty him of water and try the kiss of life. She leaned over to get a grip under his armpits. But as she heaved him up, the boat began to tilt over, and in fear of it capsizing on top of her, she let him go. He slipped from her grasp and sank silently. She leaned out again, aghast. She could just make out the whiteness of his shirt glimmering far below. She thought he might never return to the surface, and was about to plunge over the side. But slowly, very slowly, he seemed to be coming up towards her.

She leaned over, her hair falling in the water as she reached down, feeling for him. She caught hold of fabric and pulled. Over the stern this time, she thought, manoeuvring him round. Leaning out she was able to get a firm grip, and with her knees jammed against the counter, began to heave. But he was big, inanimate, and seemed as if made of lead, and she could not raise him high enough to tilt him into the boat. Sweat poured down her body as she struggled ineffectually. She began to cry with vexation at her weakness, then cursed herself, as if anger might revitalise her flagging muscles. Bloody feeble little cow, she berated herself. Surely all the rowing she did must have given her some strength? But she could not manage to produce the leverage she felt certain should be there. Slowly she let him slide back, her back and arms aching.

She climbed overboard, the water rising chilly up her body, till her face was down level with his, drew him round to the side of the boat again, holding onto the gunwhale. Then, pulling the boat over, she tried to get a shoulder underneath him and push him up, roll him over into the boat. But she only succeeded in swallowing mouthfuls of lakewater. Gasping and spluttering, she hung onto the boat with one hand and onto him with the other. She hated to let his handsome face sink beneath the surface, even for a moment. But she knew she was defeated, and wept.

Unnoticed all the while, dusk had been greying the light, and by the time she had scrambled back into the boat, it was difficult to distinguish him still floating beside her. She sat down, tired and sodden, wishing she had taken her clothes off before getting into the water, so that she would have had something dry to get into. All she could do now, she thought grimly, was tie the painter to him and tow him ashore. By the time she struggled to unfasten it, mostly by feel, and reattach it to the stern, she had lost him, and paddled round frantically searching for some minutes before she bumped into him again. She lashed the rope round his waist in almost total darkness. She was quite chilled as she felt the oars back into their rowlocks and sat back on the thwart.

There were pinpoints of light glowing round the lake now, from houses and farms, but they were like stars, she could not tell how distant they were, and could not decide in which direction to row. There was a glow in the sky which she thought must be from the town. She would head in that direction, as the southern shore would be the least hazardous to approach. A fine rain had begun to fall.

Pulling the body made the boat seem heavy. She rowed with more desperation than sense at first, before settling into a steady rhythm. She prayed she would not run into anything. The worst would be to hit an island and not know that it wasn't the shore. But mostly she thought only that she might have saved him, had failed to get him into the boat and breathe life back into that still face. Rationality would not come to her aid, point out that it was likely he had long been dead.

Faces had always been important to her. She walked down streets lifting and slipping her glance into the face of every man she passed, knowing each time she would meet their eyes waiting for hers, little secret meetings of eyes. She seemed to know most of the faces, the pathetic ones astray for mothering, the slavering ones mouthing her as flesh, hunters with a glint, the curious, the equally assessing, those who curled their lips and dismissed her for not reaching their ideals. If you were slim and had a mane of hair all men would look at you, they were conditioned to look, they were trapped halfway up the throat of their reactions. There were many times when she wished she could have pressed some secret switch that would quietly have withdrawn all the distinctly female attributes, not to turn her into a man as well, but get rid of the distractions, streamline her into the mass of exploring ideas she felt constituted herself, long before the person she was with would become demeaned into a slavering, pawing dog.

Each time she dug the oars into the water, she could feel the tug of the rope on the dead weight trailing invisible astern, and felt pain that she was jerking his body, that she was treating him cruelly, undignifiedly. She kept seeing his quiet, reposeful face, the bony resignation, and lumps would rise in her throat, squeeze tears from her eyes. She seemed to see his face as if it were carved from marble, impervious to the water pouring over it, all its thoughts locked impenetrably inside, never to be extracted. His eyes would never look into hers. Her tears flowed into the darkness. She began to imagine him alive.

There came a knock on her door. He had blue eyes. Something roughly wrapped in newspaper was held in his hands.

—I caught a couple of trout. Will I cook them for us?

His pockets stuck out sideways, clinked with bottles. No man had been in her flat before.

—I see you washed your hair, he said, as if it was a precocious step to have taken. You've a really beautiful mane.

He took the bottles from his pockets one at a time, placed them in a squad of six on the table.

—You could try washing yours sometime, she said.

—What would I need with that when I'm out in all weathers, don't they say rain water's best for hair? He laid the two gleaming fish out on the draining-board. Look. A pair of beauties. Not far off a couple

of pounds apiece.

She stood beside him.

—It seems a shame they had to die.

—D'you know, he began, tapping the rim of the sink with the point of the knife he was preparing to gut them with. I often fancied swimming down there with them.

—Will I teach you?

He put the knife down, and took her into his arms, kissed her on the end of her nose.

—I doubt I'd learn well. Maybe if I was a kid. Maybe when we have kids you'll teach them.

—Who said anything about kids, about anything like that? she exclaimed, pushing him back.

—But I like thinking of conversations I might have tomorrow or the next day, he said, picking up the knife and slitting open one of the fish. Things I might say to you like, when will we be married?

—But you don't know my answers, do you?

He laid the gutted fish on a plate, lifted his shoulders.

—Whatever happens, didn't I enjoy thinking about it?

—You are a fool, she laughed.

The handles of the oars burned in her hands. The rain soaking into the wood and into the skin of her palms, made them chafe. But she kept rowing, automatically, in and out, in and out. The rain was like an aerosol spray condensing on her cheeks, water trickling down over her eyelashes. She could feel her hair pasted onto her head and shoulders, heavy and stiff. Her jeans were like the barks of trees around her thighs. It was as if she were slowly melting, becoming part of the watery blackness around her. And the desire came upon her then, to leave the boat and enter the real medium beside her. When she rested her oars and felt over the side, it seemed warm as blood, soft and jelly-like. She would release him from his rope and descend with him, the water would suspend him weightless in her arms. Would she die anymore than she could relate to life in this plasmic blackness? Perhaps she could just transform, leave a husk floating on the surface like a mayfly, take off with other wings, follow him wherever he had gone?

The bang of the bow striking the rock was like a crack of thunder, the jolt threw her backwards, crashing her head against the bow thwart as she fell into the bottom of the boat. Dizzily she struggled back up, rubbing her head, instinctively feeling for the oars, pulling them in, as the bottom of the boat grated and bumped against stones.

Behind her were the silhouettes of trees black against the dull glow of the sky. She stepped out over the side, and stood on stones, the water up to her knees, holding onto the gunwhale to feel her way to the bow. She pulled the boat in till it was wedged on the invisible rocks, then she splashed her way round to the stern to pull the body in. She undid the painter from his waist, got a grip under his armpits and dragged him through the water, then heaved and strained him over the rocks and stones, falling twice, soaking herself again, till he was clear of the water. She laid his head down as gently as she could, then she stood exhausted in the darkness, breathing heavily. After a while she turned, and with her arms stretched out before her, walked slowly towards the thick dark stirring of leaves.

She wished she had put on her shoes first. Although the soles of her feet were numbed and insensitive to sticks and stones, she kept banging her toes into obstacles. She cut her hand on barbed wire, ripped her shirt climbing through the fence, then found herself in what seemed to be a wood with tangled undergrowth that presented a barrier she could push against yet not get through. Later she seemed to be in a plantation, the soft branches of young spruce bending like furry cats' tails to her touch, scenting the air with resin as she pushed through them. Brambles clawed at her, but seemed to pull easily from her wet clothes and damp skin. Her only guide was the glow on the underside of the clouds of the town lights.

When her feet found a gritty smoothness and her hands brushed emptiness, she sensed a certain orderliness. Then suddenly she collided with a hollow iron roundness that rang like a gong in the stillness, startling a roosting bird to crash from a nearby tree with panic-beating wings. She felt what seemed to be a metal barrel. And then, like some miracle of unexpectedness, a door opened in the night before her, spilling out blinding light. Suddenly in front of her eyes was an illuminated rectangle, glowing with bright colours, the hallway of a house, Persian carpet, barometer, grandfather clock, table with a bowl of flowers. Out of it loomed a tall stooping man.

—Good gracious, child, what's happened to you?

In three great stumbling strides he was beside her, putting an arm round her, helping her into the blinding luminosity of the hall. She closed her eyes, taking a deep breath of incredulity.

—Delia, Delia, he was calling.

A woman appeared, binding the cord of her dressing-gown tight round her waist, husks of hair falling loosely down her cheeks.

—Are there any more of you? he asked Eilís.

She nodded.

—There's a man, she began, then hesitated, wondering could all this be real. It seemed such an extreme transformation after floundering about in a black wilderness to find herself so suddenly in the warm golden shell of this hallway. She shivered.

—I think he's dead . . . . But was he? Could you bring a light? She shook her head as if to clear it. I know he's dead.

A fit of sobbing came over her, shook her helplessly, tears streamed from her eyes uncontrollably.

The old man picked up a torch.

—Look after her, Delia. She needs dry clothes and a warm drink. I'll go and see what I can do. Where did you leave him?

—I don't know, cried Eilís. I'll try and show you.

—John, you're not fit, said Delia firmly. Just come back inside. I'll go. Give me the flashlight.

—I'll be all right, he insisted. You're in your dressing-gown.

And for the first time Eilís noticed that he had a peculiar wheeze to his voice, as if air leaked from somewhere each time he spoke, and that every step he took seemed a dangerous one, not as if he were drunk, but as if he had little coordination, and managed only to walk from habit.

Delia stepped out and drew him back inside.

—It's not cold, she said. And the rain's stopped.

One of his huge hands drew across Eilís's shoulder, and as it did so the fingers clutched her convulsively.

—I'm sorry, he said. My body's a child's again.

He stood in the doorway, a gaunt shadow along the path as they followed the flashlight beam. To Eilís's surprise, it led but a few yards straight to the lakeside. There was a narrow wooden pier out across rushes.

—It was some rocks I landed among, said Eilís, anxiously.

Delia swung her torch.

—That'll be round the promontory. It's exposed to the north there. Come on.

She hurried along another path, then turned aside and pushed through alder and willow saplings down to the edge of the dark water. She moved the beam slowly over the rocks along the shore. Then stopped. Just out of its range there were other lights, and the sounds of voices.

—Could it be someone else's found him? whispered Eilís.

—I wonder who they are, murmured Delia. Come on.

As they drew nearer, picking their way over the stones, they could hear one of the voices was a woman part-crying, part-cursing. Two men were directing torchlight down onto several others who were lashing oars and several other pieces of timber together. Two women, one of them young, were kneeling beside the body. Behind them was the bulk of the rowing-boat, hauled out of the water.

Delia in her dressing-gown and Eilís shivering in her wet jeans stood a few yards away. A torch was directed at them.

—Is the boat yourn? a man's voice demanded.

—Yes, said Eilís.

—He's one of ours, said the man. We'll leave the oars back.

—Is he . . .?

—He was gone long before you found him, ma'am.

They watched as the men lifted the body onto the make-shift stretcher, then raised it to their shoulders. The small cavalcade set off, the women in the rear, the torchlight reflecting among the branches as they disappeared into the trees.

—Weren't they tinkers? asked Eilís.

—Travellers, replied Delia, tersely.

It was only then that it occurred to Eilís that she had explained nothing. It was only then that reality seemed to return a little, as they stood in the darkness on the lakeshore.

She tried to explain.

—I thought if only I could get him into the boat, I could try the kiss of life, but he was too heavy, I couldn't manage it. It got dark. It was like a nightmare. I felt so helpless.

She began to sob again. Delia put an arm round her, felt her shivering.

—Come on, let's get back and put some warm clothes on you.

The sound of Mozart was coming from the house when they returned. Eilís was numbed with cold. Delia told her husband briefly what had happened, then took Eilís into her bedroom. She had to undress her, the girl could do nothing for herself, her bleached white fingers grappled ineffectually with buttons. Delia peeled everything off, then brought a large towel and began rubbing her body all over, vigorously, abrasively, shaking her like a doll.

—This'll restore a bit of circulation, she said, her loosened hair falling in curtains over her face. You're not the first person I've done this for. The lake coughs up quite a few. Though I've never seen anyone quite so covered in grazes and scratches.

Eilís found it pleasing to be so attended to. She felt unbelievably weak, could not prevent tears leaking from her eyes.

—Sorry, she said. I haven't cried since I was a child. It was all she could say, as Delia dressed her brusquely in a capacious Angora pullover and loose tweed skirt.

—I've no children of my own, said Delia, smiling for the first time. But tonight there's two of you in the house.

—What's the matter with . . . your husband? asked Eilís.

Delia, about to take Eilís's sodden clothes to dry them in the kitchen, paused in the doorway, took a deep breath.

—He was burned. His lungs and his back. He was a doctor in Vietnam. It was napalm.

—Holy Mother of God, said Eilís, as Delia went out.

The old man was sprawled in a chair, amongst the Mozart, and struggled to get to his feet as Eilís entered.

—Please don't, she cried in alarm, although it was already too late.

—I didn't recognise you in those clothes, he smiled at her, a huge hand pushing into his wispy hair as he turned from lowering the volume on the record-player.

She found herself staring at him, examining him for signs of the horror that Delia had told her.

—I know you anyway, he added, with a chuckle and a wheeze. Seen you out there on the lake, through my telescope. Didn't realise at first, tonight.

—Did you see me today?

He shook his head.

—Other times. Sit down. Tell me about today.

Delia came in bearing a tray laden with mugs of tea.

—Don't ask her, John. I don't think she'll want to keep going over it.

Eilís smiled at her, intending gratitude for the thought, but determined not to be denied her story, yet the moment she thought of it, tears filled her eyes once more.

—Do you like your tea with milk and sugar? Delia asked.

But Eilís was already launched.

—I wonder how he came to drown. It seems to worsen the tragedy when the person is young and good-looking. Perhaps it was only the water that made him seem so. His silence spoke books.

She shook her head, brushing the tears away angrily, annoyed at her continual tendency to dissolve.

—Is there anyone we should be getting in touch with to tell them where you are? asked Delia, handing her a mug of tea.

Eilís put her free hand to her mouth.

—O God, my uncle. The boat is his. He'll be wondering why I'm not back. But he hasn't a phone.

—I'll ring the police, said Delia. They'll get word to him. He may have contacted them already.

Eilís could see her uncle opening his door to some large policeman, his pipe with its metal lid in his mouth, the few strings of hair draped across his cranium that he only uncapped when it was near to bedtime. He would grunt, maybe nod his head a few times, no emotion or surprise on his face. He might ask was the boat all right. Then he'd shut the door and go back to his copy of *The Angling Times* or *The Farmer's Gazette*. When she returned the boat tomorrow, he'd probably be down in the yard, mucking out a shed. He wouldn't stop working when she appeared, just grunt when she apologised. He wouldn't be annoyed, there'd be no grumble, no questions. She'd be expected to do all the talking. She'd tell him of finding the body, bringing it ashore. And then he'd lean the long-handled fork against the wall, take out his matches and light the pipe, before asking a question or two. She could hear him repeating the few sentences of a story he would never elaborate on. Found a nun once. Drowned herself. Fine young creature. Then he'd take a puff from his pipe and let it go out, return to filling the barrow.

—Will you be telling them about . . . the young man? she asked.

—The travelling people will do what they think right, said the old man. It isn't exactly a thing you could keep dark.

—I wonder how they knew where to find him, mused Delia.

—I daresay they were looking for him anyway, wheezed the old man, looking at Eilís. They must have seen you trying to pull him into the boat. When it grew dark they just waited for you to bring him ashore.

Anxious to distract her, the old man loomed over her, knelt beside her with a collapse of limbs, a huge hand clawing at hers, grasping her fingers.

—Would you like to see my maps and books of the lake?

He was already struggling up, turning to a bookcase. With an armful of books and maps he subsided onto a sofa, gesturing for her to come and sit beside him.

She sat down and he opened out a map, spreading it across their laps. It was large scale, showing just the corner of the lake she knew, in black and white only, but illustrating every tree, rock, marker, buoy, streams, boat-houses, islands and their ruins, cuttings to small inner lakes. She became engrossed then, working out all the places she had explored, all those she hadn't realised existed, asking questions, the old man telling her stories about people who lived in the various houses, about incidents with boats, till Delia brought her an omelette and some freshly baked bread.

—You must be starving, she said, and smiled as Eilís began to eat voraciously.

After she had taken her empty plate away, Delia came back.

—John, I think it's time you were in bed. you'll be exhausted tomorrow.

He nodded.

—You're going to have to lift me up, my legs are gone altogether.

Eilís, feeling nearly back to normal after the food, got up quickly to help Delia pull him to his feet. For all his size he was very light, more a gaunt framework than a body. Delia swung his arm over her shoulder and led him from the room. Then she came back and made up a bed for Eilís on the sofa.

—You've been so kind to me, said Eilís.

The next morning, after saying goodbye to the old man in his bedroom, his head sunk amongst a heap of pillows, and being invited to return any time she was near, Eilís went down to the lake. Delia came with her to give her a hand launching the boat and to check the oars had been returned.

—It won't tire him if I call in sometimes? asked Eilís.

Delia shook her head.

—He loves talking about the lake, about its folklore. A naiad, he called you.

—What's that? asked Eilís.

—A water-nymph.

—I'm not sure I care for the lake so much after last night, said Eilís. I can't get that boy's face out of my mind.

As she rowed back between the islands, the water was ruffled and dark, with a light quick swell that occasionally caused the bow to knock spray up across her shoulders. She seemed to see faces floating in the broken water, features peering from the shifting foam, bodies rolled past, fingers trailed through the bubbles. The waves of the lake had always had the habit of sucking down whorls of air, that spun in the depths like nebulae. Some people would imagine they were rocks threatening their boat. Odd that she had always thought of them as the ghostly faces of those drowned in the lake.

There came a sudden pressure in the air, a rushing sound, croaking voices, and she looked up at a skein of geese passing over her, their muscular wingbeats making harp-sounds. She stopped rowing to watch them. The boat pitched and rolled on the waves, making her sway as if she were dancing, being moved yet suspended by her partner. She waved a hand, restrainedly, feeling its movement would be misinterpreted by them and startle them, yet wishing she could cheer them on. She pushed the oars back through their rowlocks, pulled them through the water again. Quite soon she was in the lee of the church island, and the water became calmer. She thought how seductive the lake was. Like a lover. You forgive and make up. You forget.

Easy Advice

The programme compère was as calm as the distant woman phoning in was anxious, the two voices emerging among countless teapots, packets of cornflakes, empty eggshells and toast-crumbs, and mingling with the rustle of newspapers and the clatter of washing-up in a million homes.

The programme was for people to air their problems in the lull after children had left for school and breadwinners gone to work. The compère grew a fraction impatient. The woman phoning in was nervous of continuing, worried that, although she had been allowed to remain anonymous, her home town had been mentioned.

She was kneeling in her narrow hallway beside the small table where the telephone stood. She clasped the instrument close to her head as if afraid the slightest word might leak out through the walls of the house around her. But finally the nutshell voice of the compère reassured her.

She was only twenty-three, but looked nearer forty. Her pale ginger hair was drawn back from her forehead and without make-up she seemed to have neither eyelashes nor eyebrows; the dark pouches under her eyes made her appear slightly fish-like. She wore a yellow blouse, shapeless beige cardigan and navy-blue trousers, her feet in a pair of clogs.

The house was of mean dimension. Downstairs comprised a sitting-room so cramped that people sat with their knees in the screen of the television set, and a kitchen with a table in the centre, and as you squeezed round you dragged your buttocks against cooker-switches, drawer-knobs and the inevitably protruding sticky knife or gravy-smeared plate. Upstairs were two tiny bedrooms, the space between wardrobe and bedside so narrow it was impossible to stand upright, and if you squeezed between window and bed the curtains dragged after you. The bathroom was not much bigger than a cupboard. A small child sat on a potty, leaning his pale ginger head against the underside of the washbasin and his back against the bath, while he played with an empty tube of toothpaste.

In the kitchen a girl of about five sat humming to herself while making slow meticulous curls with a red crayon that strayed from the scrap of writing-paper onto the formica table. She was darker than her mother and brother, and had soft squashed-up features that suggested one slight puff of air was all that was needed to inflate them into perfect symmetry.

When the woman came in after the phone-call she berated the child for messing the table. Pushing chairs out of the way, she fetched a sponge from the sink, still scolding as she rubbed out the crayon marks. The little girl stared as if she had expected a slap and would normally be crying by now. But her mother had a feverish glint in her eyes and, as she rubbed, seemed to be seeing right through the table and into the distance. This the child noted, and waited to see what would follow. Her mother tossed the sponge back into the sink and went upstairs, her clogs knocking through the thin stair-carpet with hollow rapidity.

But she did slap the small boy in the bathroom, not so much because he had upset the potty, but because she banged an old bruise on her hip as she bent down to clear up the mess. She put a clean vest on him, dumped him into his cot and shut the door on his unhappy wails.

Her chest was heaving as she eased past the footboard of the bed to prop herself before the metal-clipped mirror of her dressing-table. She could not remember all the advice. Perhaps because she had only begun to take in the hope halfway through the call.

She pulled open a drawer and rummaged about to find odds and ends of make-up, several scratched and used-up lipsticks, a jar containing a smear of foundation cream, a powder compact with a cracked mirror. She sighed. It was evident she would have to buy some more.

She ruffled up her hair, combing it with her fingers to drape in differing styles, regarding herself in the mirror. Then she pulled open the door of the wardrobe against the bed. It was impossible to see anything, so she reached in and dragged out the armful of dresses. She held them to her like long-lost friends, stroking the materials, spreading the skirts across her thighs.

She took off her blouse and trousers and leaned back to try and see all of herself in the mirror, but was prevented by the bed. She tried to twist the whole dressing-table to angle it, but it jammed within a few inches. So she tilted the mirror and stood on the bed, after carefully closing a gap in the net curtains.

Bruises purpled her arms. Another emerged like a continent over her left hip. But she was not concerned with these. She squeezed the flabbiness of her belly between fingers and thumb, took in a deep breath to draw it in. She pushed at the tops of her thighs where they bulged out from the arcs of her underpants. She chewed at a fingernail, scowling, then shook the finger irritably from her mouth, and put on a slip.

The third dress fitted. It was tight across her abdomen and under her arms, but she could pull the zip up. With sudden excitement she began trying the dresses on one after the other, the bed creaking beneath her, its swaying adding to her fervour. The door opened and in came the little girl, who had heard the curious noises. Her mother threw her a blouse, and the child's expression changed from a cluster of anxious blobs to creases of delight. She was instantly infected by her mother's pleasure in trying on clothes, and she bounced about on the bed beside her. She seemed to realise that nothing she did would brook retribution now and rolled about in wild abandon, tangling dresses, knocking her mother off balance.

The woman tickled her and picked her up, stuffed her into voluminous frocks and held her before the mirror; both of them laughed till they were breathless.

Later in the morning the woman dressed the little boy, brushed out the girl's hair, took the pushchair out from under the stairs and went shopping. She went to a large store to buy make-up, pausing before the counter for some time, stroking her chin, puckering her brows, picking up this tube and that jar, putting them down, as if she had forgotten what to use. But she had not forgotten. She was only determined to budget with care. The small girl watched her mother in puzzlement, then grew bored, and was scolded for wandering off.

When she returned home the woman washed her hair and set it in rollers. Then she spent nearly an hour putting on make-up, constantly interrupted by the children who were disconcerted by this new routine. But she did not get cross with them, and they had bread and jam for lunch.

The car's tappets rattled, the differential growled, but the man enjoyed the sensation that its teeth could still bite. It was an old Cortina, kept going by regular visits to the scrap dealers. Although he spent a great deal of time worrying about it, he would always be careful to appear to be driving it with an expression of nothing but pleasure.

This evening his face was without expression, like the sand of a beach washed clean by the tide. He drove home steadily, unimpressed by the erratic behaviour of buses or pedestrians.

He wore a moustache trimmed to reveal his upper lip. There were rows of pits down one cheek where as a child he had torn at a bad dose of chicken-pox, and his eyes narrowed at the outer corners as if with a general suspicion of the world. His shoulders were broad, but a beer-belly bulged out over his belt.

Back at home, he stood in the doorway, his nostrils dilated. The house was pungent with aromas; daffodils, an earlier cake-baking, hot oven enclosing pork chops, and a faint hue of perfume. His expression hardened, with just a twitch to his mouth, as if his suspicions had been confirmed. He jabbed his coat onto a hook and barged open the kitchen door.

If the woman's eyes shot straight to his, his eyes avoided hers totally, scanning the sights the smells had prepared him for: her make-up and her dress, the table laid with such care, a chocolate cake and fruit salad, the sauce bottles before his place whereas usually he had to demand them.

Although she had tried to be sparing, her mascaraed eyes and bright lipstick seemed to shout across the table like a theatrical mask. Her lower lip trembled and colour rushed under the make-up as the realisation came to her that it all looked too crude and obvious.

The baby boy in his high-chair banged a plastic spoon on its tray, but the little girl, who had been helping her mother with the preparations, caught both parents' expressions and, level with the table, her pudgy face stiffened with gaping expectancy.

The woman tried to smile, as if hoping the gesture might soften the hardness in her husband's face. But abruptly that face broke into loud, ugly words. They fell upon her like thieves come to snatch her newly acquired wealth of hope. She could feel herself sinking back despairingly, to the bottom of the pit she had been living in.

She only half-heard what he said. A man at the stores where he worked as a packer had been listening to the radio that morning and had heard a woman from their own town phoning in to some problem programme, complaining that her husband beat her, she daren't go to the police, she was afraid for her two little children. The storeman had jokingly asked if it was his missus. He had denied it angrily, angry because he could not help wondering. Now he knew.

The woman could hear herself that morning, barely articulate into the black cup at her chin, the compère's dry voice like a pill in her ear. She said she had become demoralised, lied to the doctor about her bruises, but he had put her on tranquilisers because of the headaches and nightmares and fits of shivering she suffered after her husband had knocked half her teeth out. No, he didn't attack the children, but he hit her in front of them. No, she couldn't say what made him strike her, she kept the house clean, never ran up any bills, but he just seemed to hate her. Then came those other questions. Did she never try to please him, make herself pretty, get him to talk about his work? At the time the advice suggested hope. In the mirror in the bedroom she saw herself in those dresses, a teenager again, she remembered going out night after night, the dances, the cinema, the drinking and the sex, all in a mad nostalgia.

As she told the woman on the radio she had been too afraid to tell the police, the social services or her doctor, it had seemed ridiculous to expect them to help anyway. They were all so busy with their real problems, shops being raided, broken homes with no money coming in, children in care, delinquents, people dying of cancer, bleeding from car accidents. Her problems did not compare. So she had seized upon the hope suggested, to be responsive, caring, look young and appealing again.

The first blow caught her on the cheekbone, thickening her head with muzziness.

—Making me look a fool, he shouted. Telling tales.

The second landed in her stomach, doubling her up, the kitchen table jerking sideways, all the cutlery clashing, her elbow flying out, knocking the sauce-bottles over. The third blow smashed into her mouth, and she fell over backwards, crashing past a chair, scraping down cupboard doorknobs onto the floor, knives and spoons clattering round her, followed by plates, cups and the milk-jug spilling.

The man stepped back, wiping his mouth with the back of his hand, then rubbing his knuckles. The tomato ketchup bottle had broken and its red contents spilled over the cake, the dessert of fruit salad she had prepared lay spilled over the dresser. She lay on the floor, whimpering and groaning. The little boy had pushed his fingers into his mouth and rocked himself unseeingly. The small girl just stared, her mouth open. Then he turned on his heel, grabbed his coat off its hook, and the front-door slammed after him.

Slowly the woman struggled up, cramming her apron into her bleeding mouth, righted the chair and sat among the ruins of the meal.

As her mother's shoulders shook with sobs, the little girl remained staring, as if comprehension would elude her for the rest of her life.

Intrusion

The path was becoming bearded over with seed-laden stalks of grass.
He stopped, aware of his isolation in the midst of the green shambles
of nature. Wild clematis and brambles climbed up to merge with the
lower branches of trees, and their slopes hummed and quivered with
a nectar-hungry mob of insects. It was the first time his inner
awareness had woken to his surroundings since he set out on his
walk. He must have passed the last signs of human habitation
without noticing them, those ramshackle bungalows on the edge of
the woods, with their rusty wire fences, patched with battered sheets
of corrugated iron and old metal bedsteads, to keep in moaning
chickens and mud-caked pigs. His mind had been all on his hurt, his
bitter reaction to the rejection; going over it again and again, seeing
her eyes shift sideways after she confessed the truth, destroyed his
dream. What treacherous creatures women were, he had thought.
Let you delude yourself you were the all important significance in
their lives. He could not rid himself of the vision of her face inside
those fistfuls of sandy curls. He kept seeing her frightened alarm as
he raged after her odious preference, catching him off-guard with a
punch into the pit of his stomach. What a useless gesture.

A hot green calm hummed all around him. All sizes and colours of
bees, hover flies, wood wasps, white and brown butterflies, darted
in and out of the cascades of pink and white flowers. The wood was
a wilderness he had known all his childhood. As a boy he had come
with friends to swim in the lake at its centre. There had once been a
holiday camp there, but it had gone bankrupt and fallen into decay,
the windows of the buildings had been smashed, the roofs had fallen
in, trees had split the walls, the jungle taking over again. In other
places the wood had been more sordid, old cars, prams, burst bags
of rubbish. But the rampant fertility of the soil, the eagerness of the
nettles, brambles and elders to scramble upwards to reach the light,
eventually obliterated most rubbish. Here and there a young ash,
chestnut, birch and willow had shot clear of the lesser vegetation,

struggled up to join the few old trees that remained, rickety oaks, sparless elms, ashes overwhelmed with ivy.

He came out here to get away from the introversion of his parents' house, where he had taken refuge after the rejection. Going there had been a mistake. Against their little routines, his agonised thoughts had stood out like a scream in the midst of a cricket match. It was a house that smelled of washed dogs, small deodorised Cairn terriers that yapped like an hysterical mob whenever the phone rang. His father, glasses always on the end of his nose, collected old golf-clubs, attended innumerable dinners, Rotarians, Chamber of Commerce, Masons. His mother was forever opening tins of dogfood, giving the Cairns baths, walking them, going shopping for more tins, brushing them for shows, cursing the bundles of old golf-clubs that kept falling out of cupboards. His father hated the dogs, flapped his hands, snarled, bared his teeth at them.

The sun burned down. For the first time in days he smiled. It was impossible not to relish nature when the sun lit it up, even such a small corner. The outside world could be forgotten here. A blackbird leaped up onto a dead branch, uttering a few startled cries, its tail jerking in time, then paused, one wing half-extended to defecate, while it eyed him. Warblers trilled in the treetops, doves cooed. Was there an outside world? There was no sound of it, not the slightest indication. Only the scent of all the flowers, briar roses, brambles, poppies, buttercups, purple vetches, making the air as rich as a perfumed bedroom.

He remembered taking her out one sunlit Sunday for a picnic. They had seen a ruined castle in the distance as they drove along, and came upon a tourist-board sign beside a footpath. They crossed endless small fields to reach the castle, by which time she was complaining that her shoes hurt, she hadn't come dressed for hiking. It was a wild place, fenced off by the farmer lest his cattle should fall into the open dungeons. The walls were so shattered in places that it seemed they must have been blown up. The tourist-board usually kept such ruins tidy, but this one was very neglected and overgrown. He had wanted to imagine it in its heyday, when people lived in it, lived the desperate lives of those dark times when the country never knew peace, and they had to keep constant watch from the ramparts. But she had laddered her tights, got stones in her shoes, scratched her hand on thorns, and said it was only an old heap of stones. He had teased her that she was only romantic in safety when surrounded by domestic certainty.

They sat down on a rug and brought out the sandwiches and

bottles of Guinness from her shopping-bag. Inquisitive wasps zoomed in. She screamed at them, flapped her hands to frighten them off. Then she started slapping at a leg where she swore an ant had ventured. She leaped up and backed away, scratching at herself, brushing her clothing, cursing, swearing she had been stung. It was all his fault, picking an ants' nest to sit on. And he made it worse by laughing at her. She wouldn't let him find another, safer place, no, they must return to the car. She had looked so attractive, he remembered thinking, in her sleeveless white top and blue cotton skirt, sandy curls fallen across her flushed face, eyes glittering with pique, stumping back across the fields ahead of him, still scratching. Later, after they had finished the sandwiches and Guinness, seated in the car, she had relented. They had driven up a track, put the seats down and made love. The irony was that crushed ants fell out of her clothing, and there were small bumps on her thighs and bottom, where she had been bitten.

He turned to continue along the evergreen path, leaving the sunlit, insect-laden glade. As he walked under the shade of a canopy of trees, a bright gold field of barley glowing between black trunks to his left, he realised that he felt free of his despair. For the moment, it had gone. In sudden release he began to run. The path plunged back into the woods, merged with a track that passed the old holiday camp, now no more than a shapeless pile of undergrowth. He took great strides, rising in the air, jumping obstacles. By the time he reached the lake, he had to sit down exhausted, his breathing hurting his ribs. Daft, he laughed at himself.

The lake seemed to have become overgrown and to have shrunk since he was last there. But the water was still as smooth as glass, and dark as red wine within its green bottle. The overhanging trees kept breezes from wrinkling its surface and the sky from reflecting on it.

Only a week ago he had been contemplating death. He had imagined killing her paramour in violent retribution. Stupid word, paramour, but it described the bastard in his terms. If he had possessed a gun he might well have used it. Pointless to rush in with flailing fists. His anger needed to resolve itself in a bang, to blast the man away. But without the means, his first fury faded. Anyway, killing would be a useless gesture. The man had only taken over the baton, as he had himself before, from the previous runner. As for her, he had no wish to see in her eyes a look that saw him as no more than a brute. Revenge boiled dry, left him empty. He thought instead of his own death. The future without her was a void, a desert. Unpeopled. His friends sought to distract him, talked of their own concerns. To lose one's girl was like a death in the family, not to be talked about. So he stayed away from company, stewed in his own despair. Suicide seemed a reasonable means to achieve peace, a fading quietly away from pointless existence. He desired only a deep bottomless sleep. He could not put his mind to his work, roamed the city streets at night, did not bother to eat or shave, fell asleep in his chair. But when he looked down at the streetlamps quivering in the dark tide sweeping beneath the bridges, he felt rooted to the ground. When the mass of a double-decker bus loomed hugely towards him, he could not even lean towards it. He had asked for a hundred aspirin at a chemist's. Not necessarily to use them, he had told himself, but to have, just in case. At his digs, he opened the packet, expecting a bottle. But they were all in small foil-sealed trays, each one individually cupped. It spoiled the image he had had of a sudden swift decision, empty the bottle into the palm, cram them into the mouth, gulp them down with a tumbler of water, destiny at full tilt.

Somewhere an invisible moorhen gurgled. A small spiral of rings spread outwards from the rise of a fish. He watched to see if it would rise again. There were other sounds. He turned his head, the better to listen. It sounded like the distant echo of music, but the leaves of the trees were rubbing themselves together with an overriding sibilance. He got up and walked on, skirting the edge of the lake, and headed further into the wood. He left the path and followed a rabbit track uphill. He could have sworn he heard the music again.

The ground rose up to a slight ridge, dense with sloes and elders, and on its crest a cluster of pines stuck up like umbrellas. The music was distinct now. Orchestral. Somebody must have brought a radio. Sardonically he visualised stumbling across a pair of lovers who thought themselves safe from intrusion, apologising to them for embarrassing them.

Just below the ridge was a glade. The grass and weeds in the centre had been trampled flat. On the ground near some gorse bushes stood a large cassette-radio. It was playing *Swan Lake*. Beside it was a pile of clothes. Into his line of vision pirouetted a girl, dancing to the music.

She wore ballet-shoes bound with ribbons round her ankles, and a white costume with a knee-length skirt of tulle. Instinctively he ducked behind a branch to remain unseen, then moved cautiously forwards, trying not to tread on any twigs, squeezing between bushes, gently pulling branches aside, determined to get a little closer.

As he watched he noticed that although she danced quite

gracefully, there was something dispirited about her movements, as if she was clinging to the music rather than responding to it. Some of the time her eyes were closed. Sometimes she stumbled or made a mistake. She was very thin, and not as young as he had first thought, a long face with a small mouth, not unbeautiful, but rather miserable. She must have been a professional, he thought. Perhaps she still was. There was a marked contrast between her dancing in time, precisely and lightly, and when she made a mistake, and took solid clumsy little steps to regain her place, when once more she would become light and graceful. At each mistake she gritted her teeth and muttered curses under her breath. He saw that her costume was old and chafed, that the tulle of the skirt was torn in several places. Some of her hair had come undone from its knot at the back and fell down in wispy strands. At one moment when the music became rich with loud emotion, and she stood poised with one leg extended behind her, arms in counterbalance, he thought he saw tears on her sallow cheeks.

He could not help feeling an odd sense of attraction towards her. There was something in the miserable angularity of her face, its paleness, the rings accentuating her eyes, the bony expressiveness of her features, that drew on his imagination's suggestiveness. But he remained very still. He recognised that he was an intruder upon something extremely private. She had not chosen this isolated place to perform before any audience.

At one point she ran across to the radio and wound the tape back a little. He could not see any point in her doing so, she had not made any mistake, and she danced it over again as listlessly as before. He supposed she must be dancing an amalgam of roles, for she never stopped. Occasionally she would brush an arm across her forehead to wipe off sweat, and though she became progressively more limp, she still managed to maintain a certain lightness. Must be years of training, he thought.

After the finale, and the cassette switched itself off, she remained standing for a long time, in a sort of curtsey, her chest heaving. Then slowly she knelt down on the flattened grass, and he could see that her face was wet with mingled tears and sweat. Her shoulders were shaking. He felt he should withdraw from behind his screen, yet could not bring himself to leave.

After a while she stood up, wiping her cheeks with the backs of her wrists. She walked desultorily towards her clothes, unhooking her skirt, and stepping out of it. He turned his head, suddenly squeamish at the prospect of seeing her change. Ashamed at last of his intrusion, he backed slowly and quietly away. As soon as he was out of sound of the glade, he walked quickly, hoping she had noticed nothing.

He made no mention of what he had seen to his parents at supper. He could anticipate their disparaging reactions, spoiling the image he retained. Some nutter, his father would say, probably escaped from a lunybin. His mother would want to have her tidied up. It shouldn't be allowed, she might upset people. Whereas if he had come across some rare species of butterfly in that woodland glade, he thought, and brought it home, as he had once done as a boy, they would have said, how beautiful.

His father, getting up from the table, tripped over one of the dogs and cursed it ill-temperedly, the small creature yelping in hypochondriac extreme. This set the other Cairns barking, and his mother's voice rose to a shriek to quell them, adding to the cacophony, so that his father rushed from the room.

While he helped his mother with the washing-up she confided that she was worried about his father, particularly concerned that he might take it into his head to harm the dogs. She had been about to enter the sitting-room one day, and saw him practising with an old putter he had just bought, deliberately terminating the stroke against one of the dogs. The poor thing had hidden terrified under a chair. He let his mother talk on. That morning his father had taken him into the room where he kept his collection of clubs, to show him his latest acquisition, a driver used by Sam Sneed. Then he told him he was anxious about his mother. He had seen her cutting up sirloin steak for the dogs, and then putting a tin of dogmeat into a stew for themselves. He was afraid the dogs were turning her head.

The next morning he could hardly wait for time to pass. He sat about the kitchen, reading the Sunday papers with methodical determination, trying to use up the hours. His mother came back from walking the dogs. He found his reactions prickling when she started to complain about the ramshackle small-holdings on the edge of the woods, how they lowered the tone of the neighbourhood. It was time the council did something. Only nobody quite knew what. She began to prepare lunch, and he could not help occasionally glancing up from the paper to see what she was putting in it.

When lunch was over it was his parents habit to take their coffee and the Sunday papers into the sitting-room, followed by the dogs, turn on the television, and promptly fall asleep. So that anyone passing through the hall might hear high drama to the accompaniment of heavy snoring. He left the house.

It had already occurred to him that it was unlikely the woman would be there again. There were too many people strolling about the woods on a Sunday. But since he had to return to the city the next day he might as well take a chance.

A strong breeze blew, a steady gushing through the leaves, the upper branches of the trees in constant sway. There were people about, but fewer than he had imagined. And there were no children round the lake, as he remembered there always used to be. Perhaps children had other activities these days, conforming with what their parents considered socially acceptable, ponies and sailing-dinghies; the whole country was going middle-class. He found the narrow rabbit-track he had followed yesterday, and headed up the incline. He could hear no sound of any music. But it could be obscured by the hissing of the breeze.

He was pushing his way through the sloes and elders when he realised he was hurrying, making too much noise, and he grew self-conscious of his haste. What was he doing, he reflected, what right had he to intrude on this woman's private world? He had discovered her dancing by accident. It was nothing to do with him, he should leave her alone. He was being nothing more than a peeping-tom. He hesitated, half-inclined to allow his sense of guilt to turn him round. He stood undecided, listening for the music. But there was no sound of it. Obviously she had not returned. So it didn't matter. He would just have another look at the glade, he decided, just to convince himself he really had seen her yesterday.

As he pushed aside a branch and stepped into the clearing, he froze in sudden confusion. There was the cassette-radio on the grass. Beside it was the pile of clothes and a raffia shopping-bag. He took a step back, about to flee in guilt, when he realised that he was alone. There was no sign of the woman. Cautiously he walked out into the centre. It was bigger than he had realised. Although she had trampled a large patch, there was much more of it, overgrown with an abundance of nettles, thistles and cow-parsley. He became self-conscious then with the thought that she could not be far away, that she would return and find him in the middle of her dance-floor.

He all but trod on her. She was lying stretched out on the ground, and had been hidden from his view by a clump of grass with tall seed-heads. Even at first glance he did not imagine he had stumbled across someone resting or sleeping. There was something about her very flatness with the ground. He was certain she was dead. Yet he knelt down slowly, as if nervous she might suddenly wake, and be startled to find him there.

Her skin was as white as her costume, her cheeks sunken. Cautiously he picked up a wrist. He had expected her arm to be stiff, but it was merely limp. He could find no pulse. Her face was turned to one side. Gently he touched her cheek. It felt cold, damp, like a lettuce leaf. He tried to turn her face upwards. Her lids were so neat and round, it was as if she had been born with blank eyes. When he took his hand away, her head rolled back to one side, twisting thin lines across her neck. Quickly he bent down and pressed an ear between her breasts. At first he was only conscious of the beating of his own heart. There was the odour of sweat in the cotton fabric of her top. Then he heard the separate and distinct thud of her heartbeat. He sat back on his heels and pressed his hands round her rib-cage. It was true, he could feel the faint swell. What could have happened to her, he wondered, what could be wrong? He conjectured a dozen possibilities. He remembered her tears, and wondered if she might have taken an overdose. Or could she simply have collapsed from strain or undernourishment? She was very thin, and she was no longer young, at least ten years older than he had thought, nearing forty. But why would she be lying here in the long grass? She might have been attacked, but there was no sign of bruising or blood. No time to waste debating the unanswerable. He must get help. Cover her up to keep her warm first. He fetched her clothes.

As he spread her skirt and jumper on her, he suddenly foresaw the ambulancemen, policemen, doctors, cynically questioning why she should be dressed in this tattered ballet costume, scoffing, and he wondered if he should undress her, put on her ordinary clothes, hide the Swan Lake outfit, so that she should not be embarrassed. But suppose she recovered while he was doing it? He took off his jacket to add further covering. Then he ran.

He had no memory of that sprint, of smashing through branches, being slashed by thorns in his blind haste, his feet pounding over the ground. He knew the callbox he must reach, and thought of nothing else till his fingers were dialling the emergency digits, and his panting voice was asking for an ambulance, explaining where he was, that he would wait there to guide them. Then he was standing outside, holding onto the pain in his side, trying to regain his breath, feeling nauseous.

He heard the siren approaching from some distance. But it wasn't an ambulance. It was a police car. The man beside the driver got out. As he began to explain to him, the policeman, a heavy robust man, undid a flap on his tunic and took out a notebook. He got as far as asking his name and address when the ambulance arrived. They drove ahead, down the old track as far as the lake. There they left the vehicles; the two ambulancemen brought a stretcher; he led the way.

He wished now that he had had the conviction to put the woman into her ordinary clothes. There was something sardonic about all people in uniform, he thought. They could hardly afford pity after what they saw daily, the underlegs of life. Whether she lived or died, her private world, fantasy, memories, whatever it was, would all become public now. He kept seeing her face as she danced, her eyes half-closed, the strain, sadness, and the featherlight precision of her body that bore it. He could not tell exactly what it was that attracted him to her.

She was just as he had left her, covered by his jacket. The ambulancemen knelt down quickly beside her, opening their medical bag. He gazed down at her face, his throat tightened with pity. There was something in the balance of some women's features that always triggered off a reaction of interest in him, he thought. It didn't matter that she was older than he.

He saw the looks on the men's faces after the covering of loose clothes had been lifted off to reveal the ballet costume. But there were no comments. All four were switched into their professional roles, part laconic, part suspicious, the policemen searching the glade, the ambulancemen going through their procedure of checks. It seemed a strange termination to yesterday's scene, her solitary dancing in the isolated glade, to have it filled now with men in dark blue uniforms, and she being carried from it on a stretcher.

The policemen found nothing to suggest what might have happened. Her purse was still in her bag. The second policeman, a younger man, rather slight for law enforcement, found the radio still switched on to play cassettes. He pressed the playback switch with the tip of a biro. The orchestral music that emerged was not the *Swan Lake* of yesterday. The ambulancemen had found no marks to suggest an attack, nothing broken, heartbeat regular, but pulse slow, temperature low. She seemed to be in a coma. But there were no empty bottles of tablets in her bag, in the glade, no medicines she might have forgotten to take. They covered her with blankets, the large policeman threw him his jacket, and they were all hurrying back to the ambulance. He led the way, the young policeman carrying her radio and her clothes packed into the raffia bag, the other fending branches off the stretcher till they reached the path. The ambulancemen fitted the stretcher into their vehicle with swift efficiency, closed up the doors, and drove away.

33

Watching them disappear out of sight, he felt a pang of deprivation. The afternoon had clouded over, the breeze strengthened further, so that beside the lake it had become dark and noisy. For once the water was ruffled. Even with his jacket on he felt cold. The big policeman took out his notebook again. A youth and his girl passing hand in hand, eyed them curiously, and he could see them wondering why he was being questioned by the fuzz in the middle of the wood on a Sunday afternoon.

It was the young policeman who suggested it would be warmer in the squad-car. Once inside, with uniforms less predominant, three human faces in close proximity, the atmosphere became more relaxed. He felt able to explain the curiosity that led him to return, hoping to see her dance again. The young policeman shook his head. Never heard of one like that, he commented. You get all sorts in this wood, the big policeman added his reaction. And reminisced of youths who potted at people with airguns, a man who rode about naked on a bicycle, an old woman who drowned herself in the lake. Then their radio crackled into life, and their seats creaked as they settled back to formality. He asked if he might go with them to the hospital.

He sat patiently in the casualty waiting-room for several hours. At seven he telephoned his parents' house. His father had gone to a meeting. He explained to his mother about finding an unconscious woman in the woods, and that he was waiting at the hospital. She didn't understand.

There were many nuns, some of them with faces dark as chutney against their grey habits, with pale stockinged ankles and bleached fingers. They would smile nervously, as if men were like glimpses of banned literature. But they would always smile. He asked one where he could find a cup of coffee. There was a man waiting beside him whose little boy had been knocked off his bicycle by a car, and he explained to the nun that he thought the man needed something stronger. She said he could use the canteen, then took him to a side-door, and pointed across the staff carpark to an alley that led to a bar. He went out and bought half a bottle of Jameson, then returned and fetched a tray with two cups of coffee and two Danish pastries from the canteen. When he brought them down to the casualty waiting-room, the man's wife had arrived, and the two were sitting together, tears rolling down their cheeks. He gave them the tray and the bottle of whiskey.

Returning for something for himself he met the young policeman, and they went together. The canteen was filled with nuns tucking into plates of cod fried in batter, with large helpings of chips and peas, nurses eating salads, and young doctors sawing through thick red steaks.

They sat at a table. The young policeman seemed well-known. In vociferous mood he turned round to chaff the nurses. They were halfway through cigarettes before he mentioned that they had been unable to identify the woman. Nothing in her purse but a little money and some keys. They were concerned that she might live with an elderly relative who would now be left on her own.

Later he returned to the waiting-room. While two nurses were trying to persuade an obstreperous drunk to lie down on a stretcher trolley, a nun with a pink sugary face came up to him. She told him that the woman was responding to treatment and was not in any danger. It seemed possible she had suffered from a sudden attack of diabetes. It would be better if he came back in the morning.

He found his parents seated in the darkened sitting-room before the incandescent TV screen, watching a murder movie. They waved fingers at him to sit down quietly, emphasising that it was nearly over. On the sofa beside his mother a row of small muzzles turned suspiciously, quivered about to yap, till a peremptory hand cautioned them. He went into the kitchen, cut himself a slice of bread and spread it with the scrapings from the bottom of an old dried jar of peanut butter. Probably been there since his childhood.

In a few minutes they came out, the movie finished, his father to heat up some milk for cocoa, his mother to give the Cairns, who were jigging about the floor in anticipation, a late-night snack.

—Knew it was that preacher, grunted his father, fetching mugs from a cupboard.

—You always say that afterwards, his mother was stooping to rattle out biscuits into a row of bowls on the floor.

She had been afraid the nice black detective's children were going to be kidnapped. Once there was a circle of contented tails wagging, the air resonant with the cracking and munching of biscuits, she noticed her son eating his slice of bread. She opened the oven door and produced a casserole, offering to heat it up for him. Remembering his father's remarks, he refused the offer. He had eaten at the hospital, he told her, adding that the woman was responding to treatment.

—So you saved her life, grunted his father. Funny place that wood, always strange goings on up there, especially since the holiday camp folded. A man was knifed there one night, pinned to a tree.

His mother put the casserole into the fridge. She remembered a plane crashing in the woods, and the pilot not being found till winter, when the leaves fell off the trees and revealed him. She couldn't remember his name, but his father had been born in the house that was now the Golf Club. The cocoa poured out, his parents said goodnight and shuffled up the stairs, followed by the sheeplike flock of Cairns.

The next morning he rang his college to say he wouldn't be back that day, then took his old car and drove to the hospital. The duty sister told him to wait, saying she would enquire, it was too early for visiting hours anyway. He sat in the empty casualty waiting area. Later a man came in with both arms in rough slings. He wore heavy boots and had a large moustache. An orderly, stacking wheelchairs, greeted him as an old friend. He came across the waiting-room and slumped in a chair with a sigh. He explained with more sighs, that he was a window-cleaner, but was always falling off his ladder. He'd broken his left leg three times, fractured his right ankle twice, and broken his right arm four times. This time, thank God, it was only sprains. Realising he still had his cleaning cloth gripped in one hand, the man apologised and asked if he'd mind stuffing it into a pocket for him. He did so, then lit a cigarette for him and placed it between his lips. They wouldn't give him the hospital contract, the man complained, because the only time he'd used a cage, the cables had become entangled and his bucket had fallen out and struck a passing car. But it would have been so convenient . . . .

A nun came in, looked around, then came across. There were fine hairs along her upper lip, and she took long springy strides, fingers pinching at the beads of her rosary. He would be able to see the woman in about half an hour, after lunch.

He looked at his watch. Lunch at eleven-thirty, he thought with a grimace. He sat imagining going into the ward, seeing her lying in bed, her head on the pillow, her hair loose all round her face. Would she smile? He had never seen her smile. No, she wouldn't, she would be constrained, nervous. She would know that he had seen her costume, she would know that he had invaded her private world. He stood up, his chest tight with sudden apprehension. He couldn't face her, not like this, not across a sterile ward, other people watching. He didn't want to stumble over introductions, make her feel obliged to give explanations. He was afraid of spoiling the essence of what he had imagined. He hurried from the waiting-room.

In the main hall there was a shop. A tall English nun with a cheerful nasal voice was in charge. Yes, they could send up flowers or grapes. But that wouldn't be right, either, he thought, and apologised for changing his mind. She smiled a toothy grin and chaffed him about what it was to be young.

He all but ran through the main hall, a last look over his shoulder lest someone might hail him to say he could see her now. He found his car and set off, driving out of the town, towards the city.

In a Suburban Sitting-Room

The afternoon was hot. Every door and window was open into the kitchen where Mrs Derby stood at her sink, her fingers gently working lather through her daughter's woollen cardigan. She could not see Emma, but could hear the chattering of a small child absorbed. She had set out an old drawing-board of her own on the patio, pinned a sheet of lining-paper to it, given her daughter paints and brushes, tied an apron round her waist.

Avis Derby was in a reverie. The process of hand-washing woollens was very conducive to day-dreaming. Two weeks ago they had been in Spain, the first holiday they had had since Emma was born three years back. Stayed with her sister near Barcelona. Gone down to the beach most days. Still had her tan. Emma was the colour of a crusty loaf. Eric hadn't enjoyed it though. Except for the bull-fight. He had missed his cornet-playing. Just like him to eat something that disagreed with him. She wondered if she could put ideas from the bull-fight into her designs, the textures of the torero's costumes against the black bulls would look well in a fabric. She sighed. Maybe it had been done too often before.

The doorbell rang. She dried her hands and went through to the front-door. A one-legged girl on crutches, wearing a knee-length skirt with stiff petticoat stood on the doorstep.

—Dolly, exclaimed Avis in surprise. Where've you sprung from?

—Italy, said Dolly Daly. Thought I'd just look you up before flying home.

They kissed each other fondly in the hallway.

—Come on and have some coffee while I finish a wash, said Avis, leading the way to the kitchen. Did you come by taxi?

—I did not, replied Dolly, leaning her crutches against a wall and perching on a stool. I came by tube.

—But the station's over a mile. You're extraordinary, you're twice as active with one leg as anyone else with two. And you were the laziest sod at school when you had the two legs.

—I beat you in the hundred yards.

—You probably still could. Come on, what's the latest news, who's the latest man? When I look at all those males panting after you, I often wish I only had one leg. It's not fair.

—Who was it who told you nineteen was too young to get married?

They were chattering away, as old friends will, when there came a small voice from low down behind Avis.

—Mum. Come and see.

She got as far as saying, I'll come in a minute . . . as she turned, expecting to see her fair-haired little daughter. But the words died on her lips. Fright rose in her throat.

—Emma, she shrieked.

But was it Emma, even? Not some strange little creature from outer space? A madly coloured Fauvist sculpture. It was caked in red, green, blue, brown, only some small grinning teeth and the whites of a pair of blue eyes seemed original.

—You naughty girl, covering yourself in paint like that, exclaimed her mother.

But Dolly was already shaking with laughter, the sight was too much for anger.

—Hello, dear Emma, she said.

Avis began to laugh, too.

—If your father could see you now, he'd be ill for a month. Eric's such a stickler for order, she sighed to Dolly.

—You ought to take a picture, suggested Dolly. Any film in your camera?

—We used it all up on our holiday.

At first the teeth in the small painted face had disappeared and the mouth had begun to pucker at the signs of parental disapproval. But now everyone was smiling the teeth reappeared.

—Come and see, she repeated, as if only concerned with the significance of her handiwork outside.

—Off with those clothes first, said her mother. Before you make a worse mess. Straight into the washing-machine.

When Emma had had her face sponged back to an approximate shade of sunburn and was standing stark naked on the kitchen floor, her mother shook her head at her.

—I think you'd better stay like that. Then they all went out to view the picture.

A lot of the painting had spread over the flagstones of the patio.

—It's super, said Dolly.

—Lovely, said Avis. Both women could not help admiring the little girl's freedom of expression.

—More paper, demanded Emma. Clean paper.

—I'm surprised you've any paint left, said Dolly as Avis fetched the roll of lining-paper, tore off a length and carefully unpinned the wet painting before pinning on the fresh sheet. The small naked girl set to at once, a brush in either hand, kneeling in paint, leaning over the paper. Her mother patted the small upturned bottom.

—You'd better make the best use of your time, my girl. It's a good job Dolly's here to distract him or your father'd go off his rocker when he gets home and sees all this mess.

—You'd drive anyone spare. Why have I got to come home to this mess every day? No way am I going to stay here a moment longer, it's a mad-house, came the voice from the doorway. I just can't stand it. Emma spun round, paintbrush in each hand, cigarette between her lips.

—But Siggy, you didn't mind when I started, she exclaimed.

The sitting-room, for such it had been, had all its furniture heaped in the centre, around the edges of the floor were laid newspapers and everywhere stood oozing pots of paint. The walls were the most striking aspect of the room. They were covered in a whirling mural of half-completed figures, the colours mainly green, blue and milky orange.

—But you keep changing it, you never seem to be satisfied. And now the figures are losing their clothes. It's almost indecent.

—I'm trying to get them right, she said, frowning anxiously. I can't seem to get them to work.

Her husband remained in the doorway, the fingers of one hand pressing his forehead, pushing up into his thick Airedale hair, his other hand still clutching his briefcase, which he waved about as a gardener might gesture with his spade.

—What matters is that I haven't been able to sit anywhere except in the kitchen for the last three weeks. And I've just looked in there, and you haven't cooked a meal again. I can't stand it. I've had a hard day at the office wrestling with bloody clients. All I want to do now is put my feet up, relax, but, he waved the briefcase about again, I've got to perch on a stool in the kitchen or go to bed. It's ridiculous.

Emma stood in mid-gesture, as if moving from one decision to another. She frowned in sudden concentration.

—I'm sorry, Siggy. It won't take me a minute to make supper.

He shook his head.

—It's no good. I've made up my mind. I can't live on sardines and boiled eggs. I'm going to my mother's, and I'll stay there till . . . you've got this out of your system. I mean look at the state of your clothes. You're covered in paint. You reek of turps. I can't understand what's got into you.

—It's just that I didn't go to art school to become a housewife. I've got to have something to do.

—O God, he groaned. We've been through all this before. Paint some pictures or something, but don't wreck our home.

—It'll be finished soon, she said determinedly. You'll see.

—I doubt it, he retorted. It's getting more confused every day. He turned away. I'm going to pack a few things. I'll come back tomorrow and collect the rest.

She stared at him aghast.

—You really are going?

—That's what I said. And he turned on his heel.

She stood looking at the empty doorway, frozen with indecision. She stubbed out her cigarette-end in an ashtray, squashing it with her fingers, and sat down slowly on the arm of a chair that was filled with books and tablelamps.

He expected her to plead with him, make promises, she thought. In a way she wanted to. If he'd been a bit more subtle she might have been tricked into doing so. She didn't want him to leave. The whole thing was ridiculous. She was being stubborn and he was being selfish. He never wanted her to do anything, just be at home, keep it clean, cook his meals, be companion to all his suggestions. He hated her talking of her art school days, was always disagreeable when her friends came round. And his friends were so pompous and stuffy, they knew all the answers. Yet she always believed there was a real, human Siggy underneath. If only he wouldn't keep leaping into postures, hiding behind bone-headed attitudes, none of which she believed he really wanted. Or was she just an optimist? Maybe it was he who always believed there was a real Emma underneath this scatterbrained female who hung around scruffy galleries and arty types, who would eventually emerge, his ideal female.

—Emma.

He stood in the doorway, still carrying his briefcase, a grip in the other hand. His face seemed taut, strained. She wanted to run and throw her arms around him, apologise, plead with him to stay, cover him with kisses. He looked so unhappy.

—I'm going now. I'll come and collect the rest tomorrow.

—The rest? she echoed, uncertain what he might mean.

—My clothes, he said impatiently.

She felt relieved, then alarmed.

—You don't mind . . . leaving me alone?

—What do you mean? he asked.

—I'm still your wife, aren't I?

—Look, he said heavily. You don't seem to have the slightest inkling how unsettling this has all been. My discomfort obviously hasn't concerned you in the least. You ignore my complaints. So perhaps if you're left on your own, you'll realise. Shock treatment, if you like. I can't think of any other way.

—You bastard, she cried, angry as she had never been. If that's the way your mind works, go on, run to your mother's skirts.

After the slam of the front door she stood quivering, aware that her whole body was bristling. There was everything in that slam. Shock, outrage, pain, failure to have the last word. Good riddance. She went into the kitchen to find more cigarettes. There on the table was a wad of notes stuck under a milk-bottle. Typical that he couldn't have handed them to her directly. Her hands were shaking as she ripped the cellophane off the new packet and failed at first to get the lighter to ignite. Exhaling smoke with a long, grating sigh, she sat on the ege of the table, shivering.

They had had quarrels, never rowed. They had been like puppies, she supposed, careful not to bite too hard. But how was it she had not been able to see this coming? Had her head stuck in paint. But her work had become important to her, almost fundamental, a revival of her old interest. And she had so wanted to get it right. And it wouldn't come. Like sitting on the bog having a difficult crap, wanting to be quiet, then bells start ringing, there's a smell of burning toast, people start shouting for you.

She felt scared. Was this the end of their marriage? Just like that? The parting had seemed so ugly. He had seemed so remote, spoken so bitterly, as if he despised her. And she had shouted at him. Why did she have to go and do that?

A little over a year ago life might have been filled with unanswered imponderables, but relationships had seemed idyllic. Siggy had courted her with the traditional male display of charm, lavished her with presents, taken her out non-stop, as if life was one long entertainment, a never-ending party. She could see now that it was like the way he had described the sycophantic courting of a buyer to gain a contract for his firm. But at the time she had been dazzled by it, swept along, enjoying every moment. All so different from relationships at art school. That had been another world, groups of friends, hours of concentration, midnights of discussion. She was teaching when she met Siggy. Teaching had been a jerk into cold reality after the esoteric world of the art school. Did artists only paint pictures for other artists? Poets only write poetry for other poets? She had ceased to paint. Siggy had appealed to her . . . he still did, she thought. He had appealed to her because he seemed the opposite of the men she knew, outgoing, a whooping hunter nailing targets with casual sang-froid. He had revived her childhood enjoyment in riding, taking her out on his parents' horses. Why couldn't one have something out of all these different lives? But people seemed to separate them, insisting on belonging to one sect or another. Or was it her own dilemmas, her own lack of resolution, her searching for a role?

She felt there must be some solution, if she could but work it out. She remained thinking for hours, smoking, drinking coffee, till it grew dark. The phone rang. Some friend of Siggy's. She was flustered, trying to think how to explain he was staying at his mother's. Should she say his mother was ill? What was she going to say to others, she wondered afterwards. Perhaps he'd feel lonely and relent, come back tomorrow. Only his mother's cooking was so much better than hers.

It wasn't so much the emptiness of the bed that felt strange, it was the knowledge that it was deliberately that way, that half of it was rejected space. She had been left alone before, when Siggy went to Berlin and Rotterdam for his firm. But those had been acceptable circumstances, and she had revelled in the bed to herself, knowing that he would be back in two days, laden with duty-free perfume and gin, and always something beautifully wrapped from an expensive shop, a silk shirt the first time, a gold lighter the second. Where was it? she thought in sudden panic. On the bedside table by the radio-alarm. Tonight she alternated between shunning his side of the bed, treating it like a barren pit, and then in sudden fury spreading out across the bed like an octopus, cooled by the unused area of sheet. She did not find much sleep.

She got up early next morning, determined to work hard on the mural. She took her coffee and slice of toast and contemplated the figure of a man playing a mandolin. The subject of the mural was intended to be the seven ages of man. The mandolin player was serenading his coy love, and she wanted him to express yearning by the anxiety in his body. He possessed chin-length hair and was only nude by virtue of her having spent so much time redrawing his figure he had become reduced to simple anatomy. At some stage in her contemplation a bell rang and she hurried into the hall, before realising it was only the alarm-clock. The next time a bell rang, she did not respond, and started at the sound of a voice in the hall.

—Anybody at home?

Siggy, she thought, running out. In the hall stood a man in a cap, with a leather moneybag slung across his grey uniform jacket.

—Sorry, he said. 'The door was open. Your milk bill's one pound five this week.

She stared at him. He had the same chin-length fair hair, almost the same features as the mandolin player. Her purpose was pure instinct.

—Could you spare a few minutes? she asked, breathless. In here.

—Lord, he exclaimed, looking round the sitting-room, staggered by the dominance of the mural. You wouldn't believe such things could exist in a quiet little flat like this.

—I'm trying to get this figure right, she explained, pointing it out. You see, he's quite like you, isn't he? Do you think you could pose for me?

—Well, he said, shrugging as if helpless in the matter. I've got nine streets of milk to deliver by ten.

—It'll only take a few minutes, come on. She put the mandolin in his hands, turned him round to face the light.

—Hey, what is all this? he exclaimed, put out by the unexpected familiarity of her handling him as she put him into something approximating the pose she wanted.

—Just five minutes, she said soothingly, already flipping over the thin pages of a large sketch-pad.

—I've never done anything like this before, he said, shaking his head.

—You couldn't take off your jacket, could you?

—Anything to oblige a lady.

She stuck her felt-tip pen into her mouth.

—What about your shirt? I bet you've got a terrific chest.

—Wait a minute, what's going on, are you trying to get me down to my skin? he demanded.

—Why not? she retorted.

—Are you a sex-maniac or something? he asked suspiciously.

—Do I look like one?

All right, he agreed, and pulled off his shirt, and then in a sudden rush of bravado, tore off his trousers and underpants, as if certain such a display would shock her presumption. You asked for it.

—That's marvellous, she exclaimed, unabashed, thrusting the mandolin into his hands again. Turn this way a little, look over there. That's great.

He moved more dazed than obedient. She picked up her pad and began to sketch rapidly. She wondered if she should not feel chagrined that his penis should remain so drooping. He ran his fingers over the strings of the mandolin.

—Do you get every strange bloke who comes into your place to do this?

—Look over into the corner, she said, pointing. No, it's the first time. I wish I'd thought of it before.

What amazed her was that the whole thing seemed to have happened more or less by accident.

—You're the answer to my problems.

—Glad to help a lady solve her problems, he said. Never in all my days thought I'd be doing this on a Tuesday morning. My mates'll never believe it. Christ, look at the time. I've been here twenty minutes. The float's parked outside. You'll be getting my profession a bad name.

—One more minute, she cried. I've nearly got it. You've been marvellous. The answer to an unconscious prayer. That's it. Great. Thank you.

She put the pad down.

—I'll make you a cup of coffee while you're dressing.

She was back with two cups just as he was slipping the strap of his bag over his head.

He nodded at the sketch lying open on a chair.

—Never seen an artist at work before. You make it look as easy as signing on the dole.

—If you knew how I'd been struggling. I've put milk and sugar in, all right?

He gulped down the coffee, glancing at his watch, then shook his head.

—You may be a great little artist but you don't make good coffee. Next time I'll make you a cup. That's if it's all right by you to come round and see how the picture's getting along?

—Maybe I could use you again.

—I don't know about that. I think I must have been barmy. But there was a certain glint in his eyes as he flicked them upwards.

—I've got to go, I'll be getting my cards if the supervisor finds out.

—Tell them you had a puncture, she called after him. Wait, I didn't give you your money. She fetched her purse and ran after him.

Here, have a bit more for posing for me.

—Don't be daft, he said, giving it back. Wait till you're famous. See you.

She listened to the whine of the float departing, the jingle of its bottles, then she returned to the sitting-room. Now to get down to work, she thought, pleased at the results of her sketch. Work, work, work.

Not only did she work on the figures on the wall but she set up her easel, found a dusty canvas, cleaned it, and began a painting of her sketch of the milkman. She worked steadily throughout the day. The sound of a key in the latch seemed so normal she paid no attention to it. But the familiar sound of a briefcase being dropped by the door made her spin round.

—Siggy.

She put her brushes down, ran round the pile of furniture to greet him.

He held out the palms of his hands like buffers, backing away.

—No, no, you're covered in paint.

But he was grinning all the same.

She unbuttoned and struggled out of her blouse, pushed off her skirt, and clad in her slip, clasped him to her, kissing him with delight.

—Linseed No 5, he said, wrinkling his nose. How've you been?

—Missed you.

—Me too, he murmured, returning to kissing her, their embrace becoming love-making, so that in stumbling fox-trot they revolved into the bedroom, fell on the bed and pulled each other's clothes off. She forgot all about her diaphragm, and all unknowingly was impregnated with the beginning of her first child.

Later they got dressed and went out to a restaurant. It was after they had finished entrecote steaks, and she was gazing fondly across the table at him, revolving her half-empty glass of burgundy, that she suddenly thought of the painting of the naked milkman that he had not noticed, and paled, her other hand striking her sternum.

—What's wrong? asked Siggy.

—Indigestion, she replied.

In the morning she was up first, boiled Siggy an egg, made him coffee, had it all laid out in the kitchen, when he appeared yawning, running his electric shaver over his chin.

—Mother's food may be marvellous, he said, after consuming his egg. But it's like living in a Victorian sanatorium for fallen women. She hasn't a good word to say for anyone. And, he added with a shudder, before I left she even asked me if I'd done my business.

—Done your business?

—Her baby language for the regulation childhood crap.

—See you tonight? she asked, trying to sound casual.

—Business permitting, he replied with a wink.

She set to work with even more determination that morning. But when she moved on to another section of the mural, she soon realised it would be much easier to use a model. She wondered if the milkman would return. Probably too scared. At lunchtime she opened a bottle of wine, thinking it might give her inspiration. Siggy would be furious. Probably one of his good bottles. Siggy? What about Siggy? Why had she never thought of using him before? The perfect figure. But she'd have to broach it tactfully, perhaps seize a moment when he was starkers anyway. As long as he was in a good mood. She was filled with enthusiasm at her idea, and spent all afternoon working on the backgrounds.

Late in the afternoon the front-door bell rang. On the doorstep stood a large policeman. Behind him were two more policemen. She quailed.

—O my God, she exclaimed.

—Is it Siggy? Is he dead? What's happened?

The policeman looked puzzled.

—Is your car a blue Renault 4, registration MPW 126P, madam?

She nodded, trying to think rapidly, was it parked on double yellow lines, had she knocked anything over, forgotten to tax it . . .

—You didn't report it missing? asked the policeman.

—But I can see it, she replied, pointing down the street.

—We just put it there, madam, said the policeman laconically. We stopped two youths in it this morning on the motorway. Perhaps we could just come in and check a few details?

—I haven't used it for a few days, she said, leading them into the kitchen.

The policeman sat down, took out his notebook. His two colleagues drifted, as policemen will, quietly about the flat. He had got as far as writing down her full name when one of them appeared in the doorway.

—Hey, Toby, come and see this, it's fantastic. Excuse me, miss, you wouldn't mind if we showed him your room with the paintings?

Toby abandoned his notebook and they all went into the sitting-room.

—Hell's angels, he said, hand to chin. What's it about, if I might ask?

—It's about the seven ages of man, Emma began to explain. Only there seem to be more than seven. I'm not very good at counting, and I kept getting more ideas, and the walls are pretty big. You can see the obvious themes like childhood, courting, old age . . . listen, would anyone like a drink? I've opened a bottle of wine.

—I trust you realise, madam, that offering a drink to a policeman on duty can under certain circumstances be considered a bribe, which is a very serious offence?

—O my God, exclaimed Emma, horrorstruck, before realising that none of their faces was straight.

She flipped her fair hair back.

—It's a very innocent wine, she said, amidst their laughter.

—I don't suppose we'll come to much harm on a small glass, madam.

—Please don't keep calling me madam, she said, returning with the bottle and four glasses. My name's Emma.

—This is Frank, I'm Toby and the little one's Eric.

Eric, who was slight, not much more than twenty, rolled his eyes resignedly, as if used to being teased. Frank was tall and thin. Toby was large, slow-moving, but with small swivelling eyes. They raised their glasses.

—Lot of work in it, said Frank, wiping his moustache and nodding at the mural. You a professional?

—I did go to art school.

—That's obvious, said Eric enthusiastically. It's bloody clever.

—But you've no idea the trouble I'm having, she sighed. It's so difficult to get the figures right without models to pose for them.

—That bloke's the spitting image of you, Frank, said Toby pointing to a figure kneeling among a group of card-players.

—Like hell, retorted Frank. I don't have a pot like that.

—But I haven't got it right, you see, said Emma. It could be you, Frank. If you'd pose for me, then I could correct it.

—Come on, Frank, prompted Toby. Off with your clothes.

—Not likely, he exclaimed. Anyway, what about that fat bastard beside him? He's even got your beak.

—As far as that goes, said Toby heavily. Eric could be that little shrimp on the right.

—Why don't you all pose? she suggested. If I could put you all in a group together, that would really make the scene.

Toby was suffused with laughter.

—It's a bit out of our line of duty, posing in the altogether for the public.

48

—It wouldn't take long, she persisted. I'd just sketch you, you see. Then use the drawing to paint from. I work terribly fast.

—You don't understand, Emma, said Frank. Toby's a little embarrassed about his figure.

—But he'll look super, I can see he's got lots of muscles. I just know you've all got lovely bodies. She emptied the bottle into their glasses.

—There's nothing wrong with my body, said Toby. It's Frank who's nervous. He wouldn't even want to be seen dead with a skinny carcase like his. And as for Eric here . . .

—Don't go getting at me again, snapped Eric. I've got nothing to be ashamed of. He drained his glass. I'll show you. And he began rapidly unbuttoning his tunic.

The other two stared at him in amazement. And then, not to be outdone, there developed a race to see who would be undressed first.

—Put your clothes here, said Emma, pulling a chair clear of the central pile. Then they won't get any paint on them.

She reached in to rummage about in the drawer of a bureau till she found a pack of cards.

—We'll give you fifteen minutes, Emma, OK? asked Toby, pausing before removing the last portion of his apparel.

—Fine, she replied, spreading a rug on the floor. Toby, you sit here, you cross-legged here, Frank, and you kneel there, Eric, something like the postures in the painting, here are some cards, play poker or something. Come on, Toby, you said fifteen minutes.

Toby was standing about taking up grotesque parodies of what he imagined were classical poses.

—Fancies himself as Hercules, said Frank.

Never in all her life, thought Emma, would she have imagined herself standing in the middle of three naked policemen. It was like being a nurse involved in some therapeutic game. She stepped back, picked up her pad.

—Move in a bit closer, could you, Eric? That's it, that's terrific.

—Right, said Toby. I'll deal.

—Hey, what'll we do for brass, Emma? said Frank.

—Good job there's no mention of nude gambling on duty in the regulations, lads, said Toby looking at his cards. What do you want, Snow-white Eric?

Emma's pen flew about the page.

—If the sergeant could see us now, said Frank. He'd go bananas. And they all roared with laughter. A beautiful bird can get away with anything, he added, eyeing Emma. Give us two then.

—It's no fun without money, matchsticks even, said Toby. I'll pay anything over two pairs. You can have my socks.

We could win our clothes back, said Eric.

Emma flipped over a page and began another sketch.

—This is just great. I wish you'd come last week. I couldn't get anything right.

—If you hadn't forgotten to lock your car we wouldn't be here now, said Frank. Funny what little mistakes can lead to. I'll buy one card, Toby.

Emma had almost completed the sketch when there came a gasp from behind her.

—I don't believe it, exclaimed a voice. This is the last straw.

—Siggy, she cried, dropping the pad and jumping up. Wait, she called, running after him as he turned away. I can explain, she said, as he turned on her in the hall.

—I'm barely out of the house, he hissed, when you turn it into a brothel. I'd no idea you were like this. He opened the front-door. You won't see me again.

—But it's not what you think, she cried.

—I'm not blind, he interrupted, and ran down the steps.

—Wait, Siggy, she called frantically. Don't go off like this. I'm doing it for you.

—So now I'm a pimp? he shouted over his shoulder, hurrying along the pavement.

—They're only posing for me, she yelled.

But he ignored her and hurried on.

—Pompous ass, she exclaimed, her eyes filled with tears.

She stumbled back into the flat. The three policemen were rapidly pulling on their clothes.

—We're going to get shot, said Toby, doing up his silver buttons. Are you OK, Emma?

—Sorry about that, she said, picking up her sketch-pad, trying to look casual, flipping hair back from her face. My husband hates this mural. We've sort of parted because of it. She sniffed, brushed a finger under her eyes. But gosh, I'm awfully grateful to you. I can do masses of work now.

—I bet he thought we were having an orgy, said Frank. We'd better clear out before he calls the police.

—Shut up, Frank, said Eric, who had come up to peer over her shoulder at the sketch-pad, still straightening his tunic. It's fantastic. Can we come back sometime and see how you're getting on?

—Yes, do. She revived her smile.

—Come on, lads, said Toby. I'll have to invent the details for my report.

—Thanks for the wine, Emma, said Eric.

—We should have her up for assault, joked Frank, as they went down the steps. Getting us to strip like that. Ta-ra, Emma, see you.

Returning to the empty sitting-room, Emma collected the glasses and the playing-cards. She could still pick up the faint smell of male bodies, the insipid but erotic rankness of lions. Siggy had a quite different smell. As if he had been soaked in neatsfoot oil as a child to keep his skin supple. There were times when it pleased her, and times when she wished he could wash it off, just smell of soap, shaving-cream, something innocuous and medicinal.

O God, it was so stupid that he should have taken it into his head that she was having an orgy or something. It was one of the most intensely practical sessions she had experienced, better than when the milkman posed for her. In fact her concentration had been so intense that she felt weak at the knees. But she wasn't going to sit down, no, she would get to work, translate the sketches onto the wall. Forget about Siggy. Put him out of her mind. She pinned the sketches onto a board, and began. She had no idea how long she worked for. Only that she was excited by her progress. This was how she wanted it.

She came to with a start. A bearded man and a girl with a white face were leaning over her, shaking her.

—Are you all right, Emma?

—Harold, she exclaimed, sitting up, putting a hand to her head. Diamond.

Harold Ironside and Diamond were old student friends. She hadn't seen them in months. Siggy disapproved of them. They were both from the Midlands.

—We came round, said Harold. Found the door open, and you lying here. How do you feel?

—Isn't that strange, said Emma, swaying as they helped her to her feet. I was working, then I don't remember anymore. I must have passed out.

—When did you last eat? asked Diamond, with her whispering Mancunian practicality.

—I think I forgot today, sighed Emma. Life's a bit confusing at the moment.

—I like your work, said Harold. These figures are great, a lovely line. I'm glad to see you back at work.

—I'll go and see what there is in the kitchen, shall I? suggested

Diamond. You must be famished.

—I don't think you'll find anything, said Emma. Everything's gone a bit to pieces. Siggy's got fed up and left. I think he has, anyway.

—You can't go on like this without food, said Harold. You'd best come out with us and have a meal. It's pretty late, but we'll find somewhere.

The suggestion of food seemed to revive Emma.

—Gosh, yes, please. It's been quite a day. Could we?

They went to a small Tandoori restaurant, and while waiting for the meal, crumbling and munching poppadums, she recounted much of what had happened.

—The trouble is I'm not the sort of wife he wants. I've tried to be. But ever since starting the mural, something in me's changed. I hadn't painted anything for months. Now it's like a new force taking me over.

—But you still love him, don't you? asked Diamond.

—Yes, sighed Emma.

Harold's face quivered as if he was in difficulty deciding how to express himself.

—I've never been able to form much opinion of Siggy, because he was always so prejudiced against us. That's why we haven't been round for so long. But I'm glad we came round tonight. A lucky chance. But the best thing is that you're working again. And it's really good stuff.

—Do you really think so? Emma asked, pleased.

—You know Harold, said Diamond. Kneel on his tongue rather than tell a lie.

—You were never the Roman Emperor though, Harold, said Emma. More of an eminence grise. It wouldn't often be thumbs up or down, mostly the grey in-between category. We always looked up to you, Harold.

—He was never wrong though, was he? asked Diamond defensively.

Emma smiled, remembering.

—Only your sense of direction. You would always say in that knowledgeable tone, it's this way, I know it's this way, and half an hour later we'd be back where we started from.

Harold laughed richly, enjoying her mimicry of his voice.

—I was probably wrong about Diamond too. I thought she was a paragon, the pale virtuous lady, but she's a dragon, works me to the bone, and you know I like a quiet life.

—I'll twist your ears for you when we get home, said Diamond crossly. He's got an exhibition to get ready for Cambridge and all he wants to do is go to movies.

Emma woke late the next morning. She sat in her dressing-gown in the kitchen, cigarette in one hand, cup of coffee in the other. What was she going to do about Siggy, she wondered. Should she write him a letter, explaining exactly what was happening when he walked in? Dear Siggy, the facts are as follows, at about four o'clock three policemen brought my car back . . . maybe it would be better to ring him, except that he might put the phone down or say things that would make her cross. Or she might start pleading. No, the best thing would be to go to his office just before lunch, face him out, explain calmly. Except that he hated her coming to the office.

The result of this indecision was that she became absorbed in her work again and lunchtime passed unnoticed. She had brought out another old canvas to make a painting of the cardplayers. She decided to do a new version from scratch, as she had done with the milkman. At about three she decided it was stupid going without food and she must go shopping.

It was a shock, opening the car and finding its interior an unexpected mess, smelling of other people. Everything had been pulled off the shelf, and everywhere was littered with greasy newspapers smelling of fish-and-chips, empty beercans, cigarette stubs and discarded packets. She backed out quickly, locked it, and walked to the shops.

Coming back, weighed down with her shopping, she saw a strange man descending the steps. Something official about him, she decided. Like someone come to assess the rates.

—Hello, she said. Were you looking for me?

—Inspector Rimple, CID, he said. I'd like a word with you.

—Nothing serious, I hope? she asked jocularly, putting her key into the latch.

She lugged the shopping-bags into the kitchen, and he followed her in.

—It's about three of my men, he said, looking around. I understand they called on you yesterday about the theft of your car?

—O gosh, she exclaimed, wide-eyed. I'm terribly sorry to have kept them. Did they get into trouble?

The Inspector wore a neat grey suit, had high cheek-bones, a small moustache, and heavy flat hair that fell sideways like a fence blown over. He looked a little embarrassed.

—I found it difficult to believe the story they told me.

—I expect it's true, said Emma, quickly. I'll show you in a minute. Would you like a coffee? I'm absolutely parched.

He hesitated for a moment.

—That would be very pleasant. Thank you.

—I have this one luxury. It's really for a café, and I always either forget to turn it off or turn it on. I've been forgetting to turn it off, so hey presto, instant boiling water, two cups of coffee. Milk and sugar?

She noticed him watching her carefully and felt she must be sounding too talkative, as if she had something to hide, could not be trusted, so he might not believe anything she said.

—Come and I'll show you the painting, she said, and was surprised at his smile of affable agreement.

—Good Heavens, he exclaimed when he saw the picture. It's more serious than I imagined. They didn't mention anything about gambling or drinking.

—They were only pretending, Inspector.

—I can't understand how you managed to persuade them to take their clothes off.

It was just to help me out. I couldn't get the poses right for the mural. They sort of egged each other on, you know the sort of thing, the last one undressed is a cissy. I'm ever so grateful to them.

The Inspector sighed.

—The fact remains, young lady, that this sort of thing won't do. If it ever got about, we'd be the laughing-stock of the neighbourhood. He sipped at his coffee, then smiled, again an unexpected gesture. It's very nice. Your machine makes good coffee.

He stood examining the painting and the mural.

—It's a pity the likenesses are so good. I might never have heard about it except by accident. The fact that they didn't call in for half-an-hour wouldn't have been noticed as they'd signed themselves off to interview you. But they were boasting about it afterwards in the canteen, and one of my sergeants, thinking it was a bit of a joke, told me. To be frank I don't see it as a joke. It was a breach of regulations, putting themselves at a disadvantage when on duty. It's a serious matter, and I have to consider what steps to take.

—But it was all my fault, Inspector, she pleaded. I persuaded them. Don't you like the picture?

He put his cup down on the arm of a chair and took out a pipe and tobacco pouch from a pocket, settling himself on his heels to study the painting.

—To be frank, he said, filling his pipe, I hadn't expected it to be like this. I'm no judge in these matters, but there's something that keeps pulling the eye back. Might I ask why you wanted them in . . . the nude, why nearly everyone in your mural is similarly undressed?

He put the pouch away and took out his matches.

—I didn't exactly intend it that way. It started trying to get their postures right. Then I sort of began to like the idea. The human body has always been a significant part of man's expression of himself. The sort of Michelangelo tradition. And I like the shapes they make. Especially men.

He nodded thoughtfully, lighting his pipe.

—I'd love to put you in, Inspector, she added. You've got a lovely face. I need someone for the father figure with his grandchild. You wouldn't like to pose for me?

—My dear young lady, he protested. What do you take me for?

—You wouldn't need to take all your clothes off, she replied. Though what have you got to be ashamed of? I can tell from the way you hold yourself that you've a good body.

—You've got a nerve, he said, with a chuckle. Asking me to do the same thing I've come round to tick you off for making my men do.

—You'd be a tremendous help, she said, trying not to sound too enthusiastic.

—I'd feel ridiculous, he protested. You're young enough to be my daughter.

She picked up her sketch-pad, folded over a page, put it down again. She looked at him, as if quite unaware of the persuasive innocence in her expression.

—To my eyes, bodies are beautiful, not ridiculous. Would you like some more coffee?

He looked at his watch.

—Thank you.

As she squirted the scalding water from the small chrome tap, she imagined herself in the role of doctor that men undressed before, not to have their ills diagnosed, but for a form of treatment to enhance their egos; not to scan them for faults, but to expose sides of their being they did not know existed, perhaps for their vanity. A bit fanciful, she grimaced as she added milk and sugar. But there was more exhibitionism in people than they were given credit for.

When she returned with the coffee, the Inspector was undressed down to his shorts. He was very hairy, and a little flabby.

—I don't think I should go any further, he said, pink on the peaks of his high cheekbones.

—That's fine, Inspector.

—Now that I'm like this, you can't keep calling me Inspector. My name's John.

—And I'm Emma. She handed him his coffee. I knew you'd have a lovely body. And all those super hairs. I think I'd like you seated. And smoking your pipe. I'll find a chair.

To her surprise, when she turned round, he had removed his underpants.

—I felt prudish in them, he explained.

He was more difficult to pose than the others had been, stiff and awkward, never able to take up a position naturally when she moved him. She rubbed a hand through his furry abdomen, tickled him, made him laugh.

—Imagine a child standing at your knee, asking you questions.

—I have a little grand-daughter, he chuckled. But she doesn't ask questions, she tells me things. She's going to give some man hell.

He relaxed, easing himself in the chair. Emma changed her mind about sketching him, put her pad on her easel, and started to paint straight onto the paper with great rapidity.

He puffed at his pipe.

—I have to admire your sauce, Emma. I walk in here to lecture you on seducing my men, and here I am seduced myself.

—To be frank, he said, a little later, it's very pleasant sitting here with nothing on. I feel lightened of all worries.

—You should do it more often, she said indistinctly, a brush clamped between her teeth.

—It must be something to do with taking off one's clothes, he said. The one thing I like to do when I get home from the office is to lie in a hot bath. It's very therapeutic. For half-an-hour one can forget all the unfinished business at the office. Until the phone goes, of course.

Later when he grew cramped, she suggested he walk about. He came and stood beside her to look at the painting.

—I see myself gentle like that. But down at the office I'm supposed to be tough and ruthless. His voice had dropped to a quiet pitch. If I'd thought about it, before coming here, it would have seemed quite wrong, a man taking his clothes off before a girl he didn't know. We've all got a lot of funny prejudices.

—You've been a marvellous model, she said, after he had posed for another twenty minutes. Thank you for giving me so much time.

—Lucky I had it to spare. But I suppose I'd better be getting home.

She felt he seemed strangely subdued, chastened, as if he might never be the same man again.

—I'd only have gone home to work on a few reports. There's a lot of paperwork in my job. He raised his eyebrows reflectively. Plenty of contact with people, too. Unfortunately we seem to bring out strange reactions in people. But I don't feel like a policeman with you, Emma. Take off my clothes, and I'm just the same as anyone else. He spoke quietly, growing more depressed as he dressed. I wonder if I did the right thing. People won't understand. They'll laugh at me.

—Nobody's going to laugh at you, said Emma, who had unknowingly wiped a smear of orange across her forehead. It could be a feather in your cap.

The act of knotting his tie seemed to help re-establish himself. He pushed his shoulders back and stepped across the room. He stood, taking a deep breath, to examine the painting again. After a few moments his fingers automatically sought out his tobacco pouch, and he commenced stuffing the bowl with loosened fronds of tobacco.

—I suppose there are several sides to everyone, he said. You've made me aware of another one of myself. I should like to come back sometime to see how you're getting on, may I?

—Please do. And thank you again.

He held out his hand to shake hers.

—Thank you too, Emma.

She took his hand and stepped up to kiss him on the cheek.

Poor man, what had she done to him? She watched him walk along the pavement to his car. His shoulders seemed rounded, his gait listless, a shadow of the brisk man who had met her on the steps. Was she undermining people's confidence, persuading them to take their clothes off to be painted? If someone sheds his inhibitions in a moment of bravado, when perhaps he is not really prepared for it, could he suffer subsequently from a sort of delayed shock? Suffer from exposure?

Later that evening she was about to cook herself an omelette when she became aware that someone had entered the kitchen without her hearing over the spluttering of the butter in the pan. Her fright was momentary.

—Siggy, she exclaimed, a hand between her breasts. You gave me a shock.

She had no time for any other reaction, he was already speaking, peremptory and toneless.

—I've come to collect the rest of my things. We ought to discuss practical matters. Will you agree to a divorce so that everything can go through smoothly, without delay?

—Divorce? she echoed, hardly able to take it all in. What do you mean, divorce? Is there someone else? You never told me.

—Of course there isn't, he exclaimed testily. I assume you no longer care tuppence about me, that you want to lead your own life, and that it would be best if we were legally parted.

—But I've never said anything of the sort, she wailed, picking up the pan as it began to smoke, dropping it with a clatter as its handle burned her hand.

—Ow, she cried. Bloody thing. I don't understand why you're saying all this.

—After the orgy yesterday? he retorted.

—Don't be silly, she said, licking her burnt fingers. They were just three policemen who brought my car back. Some boys stole it. It's full of disgusting rubbish. I still haven't cleaned it out. Then I persuaded them to pose for me.

—You persuaded three policemen to strip? he asked scornfully. Do you think I'm daft or something?

—But didn't you see their uniforms? Didn't you see me drawing them?

—What I saw was quite enough.

—O Siggy, she sighed. This is just being ridiculous. We're arguing about nothing. About your imaginative suspicions, that's all.

—Don't go on trying to pull the wool over my eyes. No man could come into his own house and find his wife with three naked men and not know what's going on. I should have known all along you're a bloody little tart.

—You bastard, she cried, picking up the plastic bottle of cooking-oil and flinging it at him.

It struck his shoulder, spun through the air and burst against the wall behind him with a squelch.

—You're a narrow-minded little prig, you can't see an inch beyond your self-righteous nose. You'll never understand anything.

—You bitch, he shouted, furious, slapping her across the face.

—Ow, she wailed, clasping both hands across her face. Go on, kill me, prove the sod you are.

—Bloody hell, he exclaimed, half-horrified at what he'd done. I'm not staying here. You're mad.

By the time she had taken her hands away from her face, grabbed a plate to throw at him, she heard the front door slam. She ran into the bedroom, threw herself onto the bed and buried her head in the pillow to muffle her howling. For the first time she let herself go, sobbed and cried, till exhausted, she fell asleep.

She woke early, still lying in her clothes. The grey morning light created a desolate atmosphere, the flat smelled stale, resembled an abandoned stage-set. As she walked desultorily into the kitchen she slipped in the pool of cooking-oil that had spilled from the chucked bottle and sat down heavily in the oil, going over backwards so that even her hair got soaked. For a moment she lost her temper and screamed in childish outrage. Then, with jaw set and trembling hands, she began to clear up the mess, aware that the seat of her skirt and back of her blouse were glued to her skin, and oily curls swayed past her eyes as she soaked the oil off the vinyl floor with sheets of newspaper. Methodically she washed the floor with a bucket of foaming detergent, filled the sink with more detergent, took off her clothes and put them in to soak, then ran a bath.

Later, sitting wrapped in her dressing-gown, drying her hair in front of the dressing-table mirror, she thought gloomily that her face was still swollen from crying. But when she returned to the kitchen, refreshed and in clean clothes, the morning had taken on a different air. Such an amount of washing seemed to have erased most of the previous night. Evidence was still there, like the cup of eggs still waiting to be turned into an omelette. But she did not dwell on what had happened. Cup of coffee in one hand and piece of toast in the other, she returned to her involvement with the mural.

She worked all morning, then found she was beginning to run short of several colours. In the afternoon she cleaned out her car. But even so, as she drove off in it to go shopping, she could not get rid of the feeling of alien presences having defiled its interior, and would keep looking over her shoulder as if expecting to find someone sitting there. She spent over seventy pounds in the art materials shop, and had to pay by cheque, hoping that Siggy had done nothing to block their joint account. He'd be livid, she thought. Serve him right. She loaded the back of the Renault, then bought a bag of apples, a crusty loaf and a lump of double Gloucester. Returning to the flat with all this she felt she was setting herself up with provisions as if about to withstand a siege. She did not actually say to herself that she was going to prove to Siggy that she could do something as valid and important as he did. But an internal flywheel of intention spun her full of grim impulsion in that general direction.

The next morning the milkman appeared. He wore a grin as wide as a mouth-organ and the sight of it cheered her up.

—Came to see how you're getting on. Don't mind do you?

—Of course not. You saved my life.

He hesitated to follow her into the sitting-room, reading a predatory twist in her smile.

—I haven't got much time this morning.

—I'm not going to ask you to strip again, she laughed. Come and see yourself.

He stood staring, thumbs hooked up under his jacket into his belt, swinging his hips.

—I'd know that daft bugger's face anywhere. See it in the mirror every morning. Here, what if people come in here and say, I know that bloke, it's the bloody milkman? I don't know if I'd like that.

—Are you ashamed of your body? Doesn't it look nice?

He tilted his head to one side.

You could have given me wider shoulders, a bit more chest.

—And a bigger head? she suggested. Have you time for a coffee?

—Didn't I say I'd make it for you the next time?

—All right, she agreed, leading him into the kitchen. I say, I don't even know your name.

—Burt, he replied. After Burt Lancaster. My parents went to every film he made. *From Here to Eternity, Birdman of Alcatraz, Devil's Disciple.*

—Mine's Emma. My mother liked Jane Austen. Here you are, boiling water out of this machine, the coffee's in this tin.

—That's out of a café, isn't it? Not bad. I'll show you the way my gran used to make it. Can I use this jug?

—I'd like to draw your head, Burt. You carry on making the coffee.

—You aren't half obsessed, he commented. One track mind. But I suppose it's painless.

She returned with the sketch-pad and began drawing him.

—After a minute, he continued, sink the grounds with the back of a spoon. Then leave it a bit longer. I started early this morning so's I'd have a bit of time to spare.

—That was sweet of you.

—Where's your strainer?

He took mugs from the drying-rack, poured out the coffee.

—Of course, it depends on the roast, too. *Blue Mountain* we used to get. Just thought I'd like to see you anyway.

—Could you tilt your head up and look towards the door, Burt?

Yes, that's perfect.

—You sound just like a teacher we had. Always used to raise her right hand and make us stare at it while she explained anything.

—You've dropped your consumption of milk, he said a little later. You hardly take enough for a cat now. Somebody gone away?

—You're very nosy, she replied, concentrating on her drawing. If I tell you, you'll spread it all down the street, did you hear, her husband's left the lady in number seventeen.

She put the pad down and laughed.

—Now I've gone and told you. I am an idiot.

—I think you're very nice, he said, putting down his coffee. You don't seem very upset by his going?

—Stay where you are, she cried, snatching up the sketch-pad again. I haven't finished you yet.

—Give it a rest, Emma. He reached forward and grabbed her by the arms. Couldn't I have a kiss?

Pinioned, with the sketch-pad crushed against her breasts, she sighed.

—Please let go of me, Burt.

—Give us a break, Emma. I like you a lot.

With a jerk, she tried to free herself and, in doing so, kicked him on the ankle.

—Ouch, you cow, he yelled, hobbling and clutching at the ankle. What'd you do that for?

—Sorry, she said anxiously. Have I hurt you? I didn't mean to.

—Like hell, he complained. You did that deliberately.

—Look, Burt, I know life isn't supposed to be frightfully logical and all that but I'd rather you didn't go getting any ideas, because I don't know what I want at present. Siggy, that's my husband, may have just left me, but he might come back, and I'm still trying to work out how much I want him back. I'd just like to work quietly on my own for a bit, think things out.

—Sorry, sighed Burt. All right then, how about coming out for a drink tonight? You're working too hard. Just come out for an hour, enjoy yourself a bit, see the other side of the coin.

The expression appealed to her, with its hidden suggestion, of other ideas to find and fuel her new course.

—About nine?

His face split with smiling.

—I'd better go. Was the coffee all right?

Thinking she had blundered in not commending it, a split second later that she was about to sound patronising, she nodded quickly.

—It was so good I just gulped it down like a pig.

She could have kicked herself for sounding so hypocritical. But he didn't seem to notice, pleased only that he would see her later that evening.

If Emma had any doubts about the steps she was taking, events in themselves grew like a sudden flourish of spring. The next day she had another visitor. It was Eric, the youngest and slender one of the three policemen.

—I was sure we were for it, but there hasn't been another word, he replied to her enquiry, as she kept positioning herself to keep him from noticing the features of his Inspector on the wall behind her.

He was very different on his own, detached from the company of his mates. He wanted to talk about art, to air his interest before her. If it was a ten-mile detour way of chatting her up, when he said he had the afternoon off and suggested she come round the galleries, she accepted at once, anything to get him out before he noticed the picture.

Nevertheless she felt she had strict control of the days that followed. She was now quite single-minded about her work, determined on her purpose, but she seized on moments of going out with people she hardly knew, as if her new resolve had suddenly enlarged her range of vision, and here were shutters locked before that she could now open, not knowing what she might view through them. They also allowed Siggy to fade from her mind, a sub-conscious yet deliberate act. At times she felt scared at her new power, as if his departure had opened some Pandoran box inside her and it had changed her character into someone she did not quite recognise. From each outing she returned with fresh determination to work on new ideas. She seemed to meet more and more people.

One afternoon there was the sort of incident she couldn't help feeling looked as though she had engineered it. The plastic handle of an over-filled shopping-bag snapped, spilling the contents across the pavement; and then this immaculate being stooped from his pin-striped height to help her retrieve the scattered cans and packets, restore them to her shopping-bag, and as she gazed into his gold-spectacled face and honed pink cheeks, she saw him at once as the figure of a judge she wanted for the mural and persuaded him to escort her home . . . and there divest himself of his stockbroker's saville-row.

Yet throughout all this time she remained faithful, as the saying goes, to Siggy. Although she was desired by many, often pleaded with, and opportunities strewed themselves liberally around her, it was as if the fire of her enthusiasm concentrating on her work generated a heat that kept people back. Many of those she had painted, who returned, were as much fascinated by this phenomenon as by their attraction to her. None of them really thought of her as twisting them round her little finger when she persuaded them to pose again. Rather that she was seeing them in some special way, that stimulated their egos. And then . . . she missed her period.

She had the kind of periods that if they did not occur, they would immediately be missed; heavy, debilitating, accompanied by headaches. She debated whether it might just be due to the hyperactivity of her new way of life. She discussed it with Diamond.

—The chemist round the corner operates a pregnancy advisory service. Why don't you try them? Though I never had any luck with them.

—I never thought of that.

The truth came two days later. Positive.

After the first shock, she found herself incredibly pleased, as if it were an unexpected bonus. Except that in the middle of this new, extraordinary life, it seemed impossible to accept that the embryo within her was anything to do with Siggy; or that it had any kind of father. It seemed more likely that it had some kind of immaculate conception. She was producing an enormous output of work. At the same time was living a life rather like those heady days of courtship, being taken out continually, being expensively indulged. And in the midst of it all a chemist had handed her a lottery ticket that said she had won a baby as well.

But her thoughts did turn back to Siggy. There had been no communication from him personally, neither sight nor sound. Only a letter from a solicitor to state that she could use the flat for the present and there would be a weekly payment of forty pounds in lieu of maintenance. She wanted to tell him of her pregnancy. But it occurred to her at once that he would refute that he was the father, and claim the child was the offspring of one if not all the naked men on the mural and the paintings and drawings she was producing. She could even visualise it herself as a child of the room, the sacred chamber of her existence, with its circle of figures.

The room no longer had a pile of furniture in the centre. To give herself more space she had sold everything except a couple of chairs and a table now covered in paints and brushes. It had become her studio. She smoked a great deal, there were ashtrays piled with butts everywhere. In a pocket of her jeans was the small hard lump of the gold cigarette lighter Siggy had bought her on his last trip abroad. Often she would feel her belly, expecting to find another small lump there. But there was nothing. She remained as flat as before. Only her breasts seemed changed, in early optimism of future requirement. And she felt sick in the mornings.

Perhaps it was her mind turned to children that encouraged her to borrow a friend's daughter for the mural. But children do not easily pose, become restless when confined, so she persuaded the child to bring some friends, and drew them all while they played, or while they themselves drew and painted.

It was the sight of this particular work that first had Harold and Diamond suggesting she should have an exhibition, and then the stockbroker she had used for her figure of the judge suggested the same. He bought several drawings. But Emma only wished to complete the mural, as if some long forgotten recess of her mind still believed its conclusion would bring Siggy back. She did not wish to be distracted by thoughts of arranging exhibitions. But when Desnoyer Smith brought round a gallery-owner to meet her, she eventually allowed herself to be persuaded.

Kurt Polignac was small, with a sinewy, skeletal face. He gave off the same aura of discreet wealth as Desnoyer Smith, the stockbroker. The manicured hands, honed jowls, meticulously combed hair, were all done as if as much care had gone into his morning toilet as Fabergé would have taken with an egg. He was very restless, moving about in a manner that began mincingly and always terminated decisively, as if he was correcting himself. He was courteous, but somewhat put out at being placed in the position of trying to persuade someone unknown that he wanted to show her work. And he was irritated with his friend, who kept taking away his ground.

—It's different, yes, he agreed, trying to make it sound only the slightest advantage.

—You've always said, Kurt, that it was time for a return to figures with charm, said Desnoyer Smith enthusiastically.

—Perhaps, he agreed, arching his mouth. But men . . . so many men. Men are not very appealing to men, except to a rather limited minority.

—But you said the other day half your customers were women nowadays, Kurt. And you must admit they're very romantic figures. She gives them a sort of timeless quality. Sorry, Emma, to talk about you as if you weren't there.

Polignac was a little acid with Desnoyer Smith after they left.

64

—But I'm on her side, old boy, said Desnoyer. Surely she needs allies more than you do, you old reprobate.

—I have to admit that she is both charming and talented, and it will be a pleasure to exhibit her work, possibly even profitable, so I forgive you. But if such an occasion arises in the future, I will go on my own. It's ridiculous only taking 25% when you know 33% is our standard. You'll give me dinner for that.

—My pleasure, but not tonight. The old lady's got her Irish father over and his singing would offend your aesthetics.

—I saw Dolly a few days ago, said Polignac. Always an unforgettable sight, the way she flies along on her crutches.

—Yes, sighed Desnoyer Smith. I think she enjoys causing a stir. One-legged women aren't that common.

As the weeks passed, Emma gradually finished the mural, but she was working on so many other projects at the same time that its completion was hardly noticed. Her largest venture was an entire football team she captivated into stripping. Instead of seating them in the usual group of three rows, she had them standing about in a variety of poses she divined indicated some characteristic of each individual. She put them on a huge canvas, and Kurt Polignac called to visit her, muttered something about the Night Watch, very excited, rushed out and returned with a large bunch of roses. It was a mistake, or had he half-hoped it would happen all along? She was carried away by an idea on the instant, and persuaded him to pose, bearing the roses.

During this time as she gradually swelled with child, her belief that Siggy would one day reappear, appreciate his mistake and come back to her, reasserted itself. She did not visualise this in practical terms, but more as young girls used to dream of knights in shining armour coming to rescue them from their adolescent confinement, a hazy conception in the backs of their minds, a subject to daydream with, forgotten as soon as thought of. She was far too busy to think about it seriously, never for a moment planned ways of encouraging him to return, nor did anything to call his attention to what she was achieving. She didn't even ask herself whether she really wanted him back. Yet his image remained strong enough to deter her from forming any other than friendly relationships. Many of her friends seemed far more concerned than she that she was about to produce a child, living on her own. Meanwhile she attended a pre-natal clinic. She followed a prescribed diet sheet. She even gave up smoking.

Polignac had decided to alter his schedule of forthcoming exhibitions to fit her in far sooner than he would normally have done, an honour of which she was quite unaware. It was, of course, a shrewd sense of business that impelled him. This was an exhibition whose ripeness he assessed could not be delayed. He spent a good deal on publicity.

Emma was seven months pregnant the day Desnoyer Smith called to take her to the opening. She was busy working when he arrived, having forgotten all about it. He had to laugh. He had grown very fond of her.

—What drives you, Emma? What makes you go on working like this? he asked, standing in the hall while she changed in the bedroom.

—I could invent lots of answers, she replied, wriggling into her maternity dress.

—I know all those, he said. What's the real reason?

She appeared in the doorway, brushing her hair.

—My mother told me I painted all day, week after week as a tiny child. Sometimes it's as if there's some kind of energy coming from outside me, that I'm just a part of. With Siggy I began to feel small. I don't mean that I feel big now. She laughed. Apart from this. But I was leading a nothing life, swept along in other people's wakes. Now all of me seems to be in use. I know that doesn't really explain anything. Probably there aren't any simple reasons.

He nodded.

—I don't suppose I expected any Paulian revelation. Come on, we're late already.

—I haven't put any make-up on yet.

—You don't need any. I suppose it's something to do with maternity, but you're glowing like a rose. Not that you're not always a delight to the eye.

She gripped his arms to rise on her toes and kiss him.

—You're very sweet. Where's my bag? Come on, we'll be late.

The exhibition was a revelation, almost a shock to her. All her paintings and drawings that had been in stacks against the walls and heaps on the floor of her studio, were now in handsome frames, given space to themselves upon bland velvet walls, so that they seemed like jewels on display, half-obscured by the enormous throng of richly dressed people. Faces materialised out of the crowd, came towards her, smiling, congratulating her, all her models unrecognisable in smart clothes, calling her name, kissing her cheeks. Harold of all people in a suit. She hardly knew what she was saying, nodding and smiling back, trying to answer questions, when she saw across the room . . . Siggy. All the months passed fell away, the people between them vanished. He was smiling, too. He looked just the same, as if nothing had changed.

—Doctor Livingstone, I presume, she said.

—How are you, Emma?

—Great, thanks, Siggy, how're you?

—I was amazed to get your invitation. He could not take his eyes off her waist.

—Even more amazed to see all this . . . He waved a hand round the pictures, lost for a word.

—Work? she suggested.

—You must have worked hard. His glance fell back to her girth. Is the father . . . here? He nodded at her middle, then looked round the pictures.

—I never managed to get him to pose, she replied.

He nodded, as if not really interested.

—I see by the red dots you've sold quite a few already.

—I'll miss them. But I suppose I can't keep them all.

—I presume you'd like a divorce?

—I don't know. She wished she did not feel so dispassionate, that he did not seem so like a wooden effigy of himself.

—Have you got someone else? She felt detached from the question, as if the answer would merely be a statistic.

—No. I thought you'd contact me.

—I expected you every day, she retorted. I never thought of you as far away. After all, it was only a stupid misunderstanding.

He shrugged, staring at her waist, and swallowed as if about to say something he was unhappy about. Then he cleared his throat, changed colour and frowned.

—Do I know the father?

—Not very well I should say, she sighed. You are, you idiot.

He clucked in sudden exasperation.

—How could I be? I haven't seen you for nearly a year.

—Seven months.

He whirled round.

—But what about all these? Those men I caught you with. You couldn't possibly have got all these people to strip for you for nothing. You've made them look as if they've just got out of bed. His voice was rising. I should have known you'd try to make the child out to be mine.

—Don't shout, Siggy, she said calmly. All right. I won't insist it's yours. But then you'll never know, will you? You'll never be certain.

He came close to her, his head tilted down, his mouth twisted to enunciate angrily.

—I know it isn't mine. We planned not to have one. You always took precautions. But the moment I leave you, you go to pieces, sleep with all and sundry, and this is the result.

She felt very tired, quite faint, would have dearly liked to sit down. She was confused as well. Why was this happening like this? Why couldn't he accept the truth? Perhaps it didn't matter anymore. All she wanted was to sit down, get Burt or Desnoyer to rub her back. It seemed ridiculous to be having this somehow predestined and disillusioning scene amongst all her friends and her paintings. This moment of failure had nothing to do with them. This should be a moment of culmination. If only she could get through to him. It should be so simple. They were so close. They had swung towards each other like two acrobats, clinging to their trapezes, each unwilling to let go, fly across the intervening space into the other's arms, afraid because neither could remember who was to fly and who was to catch.

—Siggy, she began quietly, putting a hand upon his arm. It really is . . . but she felt so faint she could not continue, needing all her strength and concentration to remain on her feet. There came a voice from behind her.

—For God's sake, man, can't you see she's going to pass out?

She was vaguely aware of being carried through the throng, someone saying, Excuse me, excuse me, then of being outside in cool darkness.

—Take deep breaths, lean against me, relax, take deep breaths, Desnoyer was saying, and his words impelled her to suck in the clear reviving oxygen.

She felt it spill inside her, clean her body like thirst-quenching draughts of cold water. She shook her head to clear it, looked around her. She was seated on a wooden bench in a small garden illuminated by light pouring out from big glass doors at the rear of the gallery. It was all green plants, no flowers, just flagstones, sculptures and a fountain; enclosed by the backs of tall office blocks. Above was the purple air of night. There were several people round her, anxious for her. One was a woman she did not know, on crutches. There was no sign of Siggy.

—How're you feeling? asked Burt, kneeling beside her in his best Travolta trousers and white shirt.

—All right, thanks, she replied, ruffling his hair. I think I'll just sit here for a bit, though. You go in and enjoy yourselves.

They left her. Everyone except the woman on crutches. She sat down awkwardly beside her, putting her crutches down on the flagstones. With the sort of shiver a spider racing across the back of one's hand causes, or the unexpected brush of a fingertip across the clitoris, Emma noticed from the fold of her dress that she had only one leg.

But at that moment tears began spilling uncontrollably down her cheeks, as if their level had been steadily building up, unnoticed. When the woman, with sure instinct, put an arm round her, Emma laid her head upon her ample scented breasts and wept as if she were vomiting up her emotions, deep vacating sobs that left her as limp as if she had been filleted. The comforting hold of the arms around her remained, the soft breasts she lay against and her own cheeks mingled in the wateriness of her tears.

—I'm better now, thank you, she said, sitting up. I'm sorry. I suppose I kept putting off accepting the truth.

—It's something we all do, said the woman, handing her a handkerchief.

—It was over months ago, really, said Emma, dabbing her eyes,.

—I should have introduced myself, said the woman. I expect you realised I was Desnoyer's wife. I went to school with your mother. A long time ago. I was Dolly Daly.

Emma blew her nose, blinked several times, blew her nose again.

—She often talked about you.

—I like your pictures very much, said Dolly. I remember when you were a tiny child you were always painting. You used to get into such a mess that your mother would take all your clothes off before you started, to save on the washing.

Emma smiled.

—I don't remember that.

—Is it really over, your marriage?

Emma nodded.

—In a relationship one changes, doesn't one? Adapts to meet the other person. Some sides of oneself get suppressed, maybe hidden characteristics emerge. When Siggy left I didn't revert to the old me, I changed again, went on to being somebody different. I hadn't thought about it before. Silly, really.

—How do you feel about it now?

—Relieved. I can't tell you.

—Shall we go back in? It's getting cold out here.

Emma leant on one knee, it being the easiest way for a person of her girth, to pick up her crutches for her.

The Horseman

It was a day so still that even a falling leaf hit the ground with an audible scrape. Like skeletal strippers the trees were about to shed the last of their apparel, though there was little left unrevealed. The pale clear light made the damp road shine like pewter.

The priest had been pushing his bicycle up the hill and now paused a moment to regain his breath before mounting the saddle again. He was not by nature a sociable man and used a bicycle in order to make himself more accessible to his parish. A priest in a car is isolated, shut up in a glass case, travels too fast to stop, can only wave, better to leave it behind in the yard at the manse, and use it only when time and distance needed shortening.

For a while as he stood looking round, admiring the woods, it seemed his only company was similarly garbed, two blackbirds and a treeful of rooks, providing treble and base discordance respectively. But the longer he stood the more he became aware that the woods were alive with quick movement, flashes of wings, twinkling of feet, small alert eyes. Thrushes, sparrows, a magpie, a jay.

Just to his right a path ran through the trees, straight and wide for a hundred yards before turning out of sight. To his surprise he saw a young woman standing with her back to him, about forty yards down the path. She was beside a tree and seemed to be using it to mask herself from something she was observing further away. He assumed she was young because of her thick dark hair over her shoulders, and her dress, tight leather boots, a wide floral skirt and long black cardigan. And then he thought he recognised her. Her husband had bought the old house that these woods belonged to. She had smiled at him in the village when calling into the shop. He remembered small pointed features, with enormous eyes that seemed at first mournful and gloomy with introspection, until she smiled, when her whole face became a classroom of happy children. And from that smile onwards he had thought of her as a lovely young woman. He did not know if she and her husband were Catholics. They had not come to Mass.

He had called twice. The first time there were only builders working there. The second time there had been no reply, although a car stood outside the door. Locals said she liked walking. His housekeeper said that rumour had it she was an actress and had suffered a nervous breakdown. She did nothing else but go on long walks because the doctor said fresh air and exercise was what she needed. Rumour wasn't sure the two were married. The man was said to be an antiques agent for some big auctioneers, and was always travelling. Left her on her own many a night.

As the priest watched, it occurred to him that he was doing the same as she, spying on someone else. Not wishing to appear inquisitive, he was about to mount his bicycle and carry on, when she moved out cautiously from behind the tree and began to walk along the path further into the wood, with slow deliberate strides, the forward thrust of her thighs swinging her skirt out sideways. It was as if she were stalking something she knew she had the ascendancy over, like someone coming up behind a friend to give him a surprise. But then she slowed, her shoulders sagged, and she stopped, tilting her head to one side. When her shoulders rose and fell, it seemed as if she were sighing in disappointment.

The priest remembered he had been told she was an actress and thought perhaps she was rehearsing some scene with herself, and so felt doubly embarrassed to be spying on anything so private. Quietly he pushed his bicycle till he was out of sight, then mounted it and quickly pedalled away.

The old house in the woods was very old, some of it had been a mediæval keep, though nothing of that remained on the outside. Only within did one come across walls five feet thick, a small spiral stone staircase, a vast fireplace in which one could have parked a car, with a huge stone coat of arms above it. Parts of the house were unusable, with soggy floorboards that smelled rank with rot. Other parts stood deserted, large empty rooms that the sun would enter like the auditorium lights switching on to an empty yet expectant set. From outside there were many tall Georgian windows, half-obscured by massive swags of wistaria and climbing roses. But they did not constitute a picturesque and romantic vision, rather added to the neglected appearance of the house, for half their growth was dead or had collapsed. Everywhere the grounds were overgrown, so much so that some of the house had disappeared from view, behind immense tangles of laurel and Virginia creeper, and trees had closed in round the wings. It had been on the market for years, an uneconomical, dead white elephant, surrounded by nearly three hundred acres of decayed woodlands, from which every commercial tree had long been purloined, and which provided the village with a pillage of firewood.

The builders had been to patch the roof, install some functional plumbing, and glaze broken windows. Anne-Marie had never believed she and Henry would stay for long. But she liked the isolation, the large, empty and peaceful rooms. She enjoyed imagining all the people long since dead who had inhabited them. For she herself could feel no future. Not since . . . no, the doctor had said, whatever else you do with your mind, don't let it dwell on that, put it right away, lock it up, forget about it. But who has a water-tight mind? How can one prevent thoughts leaking in? Luckily there were few reminders in a place such as this. Life had been so busy once, there had never been time for contemplation. Yet what exactly had one been doing that ate up every moment? For here, with masses to be done, the house to clean, repaint, organise, the garden to attack, she found in the end she did nothing. Not because of lassitude or depression, but because it seemed sacrilegious to disturb the decay and neglect. It was almost beautiful. Her eyes constantly roamed over it all, taking it in, as much as she could, new discoveries every day, like studying a Breughel flower painting, or listening to a Mozart Requiem over and over again. But she did fill in cracks. They were a little too disturbing to abide. And she would sometimes clear weeds away from choking some half-crippled shrub or perennial flower, to let them recover. She collected firewood to burn in the great fireplace. It was like a ravenous beast and would crunch up and consume logs as she might eat a biscuit. But above all she just liked to wander, through the house, looking out from every window, imagining scenes people might have seen centuries before, and through the woods, the greatest asset of the place to her mind.

The woods could never be called a forest, more tangles of brambles fighting elders and blackthorn, a few young beeches and ash, and here and there a straggly old tree still looming above them. And everywhere were rotting, moss-covered stumps. From a distance they still looked like woods, but once inside, the sky was generally clear above all the time; though there were a few thick clumps of trees, usually in more inaccessible places such as across a swamp or on a strip of land between two lakes, sometimes on a knoll. Some of the trees had fallen and lay reduced to little but a trunk by the firewood seekers. Perhaps it was they who had beaten out the paths, though never once had she seen anyone, except on the couple of bigger tracks that were rights of way.

She particularly enjoyed the way the ground was so unpredictable, up and down, small hills, steep gullies, lakes, a confused switchback landscape that would always surprise her with its changing views. It seemed like a land designed for walking in.

She never thought back on her previous life. It seemed to her now that she had always lived here, that she had always lived with Henry. When he returned from one of his trips he would trill the car horns as he entered the gates, and, if she were far away, she would hear the sound faint in the distance and become stirred with excitement as if it were the horns of huntsmen from centuries back. But then she would remember it was only Henry, and would start to return, for he always brought something back; he liked to return like an exotic traveller laden with wine and cheese and usually a piece of furniture or china picked up somewhere, unwanted, often damaged, but always beautiful. He had an eye for such things, as a kestrel has for shrews and beetles in the grass. A mahogany chair, a small drop-leaf table, a mirror, the wood filthy or faded, or covered in brown paint, a battered silver sauceboat, a chipped Rockingham dish. When she thought of what he might bring she would hurry, but when she thought of the way his rather round eyes would look at her while they ate supper, and the way her body would fill with the flavours of rice, goulash, salad, Brie, Gorgonzola, Medoc, and she heard her giggles as he slipped an arm round her waist for ritual retreat up the main staircase, his hot moist mouth on her earlobes, and they shed their clothes quicker than any butterfly can emerge from its chrysalis, ready for the silken toil upon the mattress, it was then that she slowed her stride. For it was afterwards, while he slept beside her like some huge warm fish, that she neared something she dreaded. It was like an empty pit pressed close against her, forcing her to look down into its depths, as she seemed to remember as a child the china chamber-pot her grandmother brought up to her face and the voice saying, be sick in this. Only now the space inside the pit opened out into an immense five-hundred foot deep quarry and it drew her towards it, wanting her to fall into it and be trapped at the bottom of its desolate emptiness forever. And all the nightmare screams she possessed came rushing up her throat, struggling with each other for egress, so that she clapped her hands across her mouth. The only thing to do was to switch on the light, to find some clothes, a gown, even her fur coat by itself, and get away, out into the night. Yet she was still practical enough to bring a torch, unless

73

the moon was out. Sensible enough to stab her feet down inside the looseness of her wellingtons. Sometimes the wind would blow her in the darkness, hurry her about the woods. Sometimes it was so quiet, so peaceful, that she seemed to drift.

Silly girl, Henry would say in the morning, his eyes fond, yet formal, as if even they always wore a waistcoated suit. He never knew what to say, poor Henry, he was always stuck halfway inside himself, could never release the strictures of his neat upbringing, though she could see him struggling to. Yet why should his tight limits of expression always make her shiver? They were a barrier she could not bring herself to surmount. So he put on his white work-coat and stripped paint off furniture, sanded and polished, till the wood glowed as if loved. Or he tinkered with his car, till its engine purred. And she would wait, a pressure from her throat down into her chest like a clumsy spear of wood about to impale her. She would approach him with a cup of coffee like Perseus nearing the Gorgon and would almost drop the cup with fright when he turned his grateful smile upon her. For so simple was his face, so innocent of anything but adoration.

In two or three days he would leave again, would step up for a farewell kiss like a boxer about to deliver a volley of punches, yet clasp her instead as if it were for the last time, before he mounted the steps for his execution. And she would wave, a small girl gesture, formal and restrained, waiting to see what was expected, what would result, and she would be left standing in the portico as limp as string. When all sounds of his departure had faded, a gale of relief would sweep through her veins, fill out her limbs, sail her blithely wherever she felt the inclination, through the house, down the paths, beneath the trees, beside the overgrown lakes.

One day she saw a horseman in the woods.

People in that part of the world did not care overmuch for sartorial elegance. Young men might put on a sharp suit for a Saturday night dance, old men wore dark blue suits of baggy serge on Sundays. But most of the time people wore overalls or clothes that would not have gone amiss on a scarecrow. The horseman was beautifully dressed. He wore a long tight-waisted jacket of chocolate-brown tweed, black boots and kid gloves. He wore no hat, so that she saw his head quite distinctly, held at an angle as he restrained his dark bay at a slow, collected canter. His profile was cut from wedges of brow, nostrils, moustache and chin, his expression determined yet abstracted, his dark hair ran in a cone down his neck. And then he was gone. But his image remained. She could not rid herself of it. She saw it in her mind's eye on her walks, when she closed her eyes to sleep at night. She kept hoping to see him again. A few days later she asked in the village shop if anyone knew of such a rider. The grey-haired, bespectacled lady behind the counter shook her head, her round cheeks crinkling their fissures deeper. She said there was a man with some race horses about five miles away. But nobody would ride in the woods, too dangerous, rabbit holes, swampy patches, fallen logs, too easy to break a leg.

The next day while halfway up a knoll in the woods, she heard the jingling of the bit, the thud of hooves coming closer. Round some bushes they came face to face. The man neatly turned the horse to pass her, raising his crop in salute, and going swiftly on his way. She turned to watch him disappear and wondered why she had not spoken.

She felt certain that he had smiled, yet all she remembered was the penetrating dark of his eyes. They had bored into her, drawn her upwards, consumed her, lashed her, sucked her dry, left her trembling. But on the way back to the house, she began to think that perhaps that was what she had wanted his eyes to do to her, simply because his appearance appealed to her. But from his point of view his eyes could have been otherwise engaged, preoccupied even, so that they had plunged into her as if he and his horse had accidentally stumbled into a muddy hole, struggled frantically to escape, to escape from her. Or was there a touch of guilt in his eyes? Yet still she felt the sensation of having been searched; his eyes had rifled her mind like a thief, and had seen, all in that brief moment, had seen, what had he seen? What had she wanted to find when she stared back into his? She argued with herself on these lines all the way back to the house. Once inside she wanted to look in a mirror, to try and see what he had seen, to see if her own eyes could tell her what she had wanted to see. But she soon realised after regarding herself that she could not re-enact the scene. Her own eyes looked back at her like a freshly arrived audience at a theatre, waiting for what was to come.

When Henry returned that evening, she became very tense. So much so that any attempt to rationalise her feeling seemed to threaten her with disintegration. But when she looked at him, where, she asked herself, could the crisis stem from? He seemed that night to be exceptionally endowed with ordinariness, going out of his way to stress his flat-footed walk, to accentuate the roundness of his face, those little courgette fingers, his habit of blinking rapidly just before making a pronouncement. He seemed only interested in talking of the most banal subjects, about the new petrol tax putting up the cost of his motoring, about a pain in his little toe and how his mother used to suffer the same, and a stain from linseed oil he couldn't remove from his cords. She forced herself to remain controlled while setting up their little evening routine, cooking the veal he had brought, laying the table, sitting down after serving the food, listening while he pattered on about a project for finding a man to do some digging in the old walled garden. She thought the wine might relax her and gulped down two glassfulls, and grew irritated that her hair kept falling across one eye. But when it came to mounting the staircase, arm-in-arm, she could bear it no longer, pushed him aside and fled into the night.

She did not go far. She had no torch and there was no moon. Later she returned, her mind a confused jumble of contradictions, and fell asleep on the sofa. She dreamed of the horseman. He was calling her. But he had the high-pitched voice of a bird. The next day it was obvious that Henry was disconcerted, torn between his natural patience and a degree of uncomprehending frustration. All she could do was to steer herself with care, hope for calmer waters. She was afraid her state of mind was beginning to hark back to the disaster that had brought them there, the matter she had so successfully kept out of her mind so far. But during the day a phone-call came, and Henry had to leave. As he drove away, she felt that at least everything was safe for the present, even felt glad for his sake.

She saw the horseman four times during the next few days.

The priest propped his bicycle against a pillar of the portico and rang the bell. Then he knocked. He looked round him while he waited. A naturally tidy man, it amazed him that the place remained so neglected, that these people seemed to do nothing to improve it, they didn't even mow the grass. As there was no answer, he was about to turn his bicycle when the young woman came from the woods towards him. She was wearing jeans, an old goatskin coat and a long woollen scarf. Her smile filled him with warmth. She seemed a little breathless and excited, her eyes kept darting into his as if she had something to tell as she invited him in for a cup of coffee. He sat down on a huge old wicker-backed sofa, with gilded feet and soft cushions, an extraordinarily elegant piece, he thought. They had some nice pieces of furniture. As she put the cup into his hands she told him that she kept seeing a horseman in the woods, riding through, and asked if he knew whom it might be.

The priest was puzzled, could think of no one who fitted the description. She told how she saw him nearly every day, that at times he seemed to be looking for somebody, and how he always appeared to avoid her. The priest said he would enquire for her, somebody was bound to know who the man was. As he was leaving, she told the priest she would like to come to his church, although she was not a Catholic. She had seen it from a hill in the woods, a plain stone building beside some ruins, and surrounded by a curiously bumpy graveyard, as if the modern head-stones had been set amongst the mounds of long-buried giants.

The priest rode away with the pleasant feeling of having been in the company of someone it was rare to be with. And it was not, he corrected the accusing finger, anything to do with the fact that she was a very pretty young woman. She was one of those people who made you feel you were somebody, your thoughts were significant too, you were not just a person to swop a few remarks with. His legs kicked his bicycle up the hill towards the manse with unusual ease. But there was definitely some tragedy behind her eyes, he reflected, an inner melancholy that she floated on like a small frail boat crossing a deep and dark stretch of water.

As Anne-Marie watched the priest's stocky figure hunch over his handlebars and his short legs grind with effort to impel the machine forwards, out of sight round the laurels, she was reminded, by contrast, of the easy grace of the horseman cantering through the woods. It was as if he rode through her mind, though she had seen him stationary, silhouetted on a rise against the sky, and by the shore of one of the lakes, looking across. Once she had tried to approach quietly and unseen, but he must have heard her coming, for as she breasted the slope of the rise there was no longer any sign of him. She had thought of things to say, of inviting him to have coffee with her. There were some old stables that he could have put the horse in. But always he seemed to prefer to remain solitary, to avoid communnication. Yet why did he continue riding in the woods, knowing that she frequented them too?

The answer could have come the very next day. For as she saw him trotting slowly down a slope, he turned his head and looked back at her, reining in the horse as it reached level ground. She thought that he pointed with his riding-crop towards the largest of the lakes, as if to suggest he would meet her there. He cantered away in the opposite direction, but she needed no further bidding but hurried towards the lake. As she ran down an incline to the thick ring of bulrushes that circled the lakeshore, she heard the swish of the horse's hooves as it came through the fallen leaves beneath a clump of bare beeches. He pulled up and was adjusting his reins as if about to dismount when, just as she came up to him, he turned to stare out into the waters of the lake. As if unaware of her presence, he abruptly tightened his heels. Immediately the horse reared up on its hind legs, pawing the air high above her. As she cried out, afraid it would crash down on her, she tripped and fell on her face. By the time she had got to her knees and stood up, there was no sign of him.

She sat down on a log, even though the air around the lake felt exceptionally cold. She had had a strange sensation when he looked down at her. Her head buzzed, rang even, as if he were crying out at her to do something, willing her, only there had not been time for any message to be formed between them. He could have a speech impediment, she reflected, though she had thought she had heard him address words to his horse, stroking the bay between its ears, slapping its neck. In some way she felt bound to the man, yet not in any way that enabled her to know or even imagine the course she should take, or what it signified. Could she say she was in love with a man who rode a horse about her woods, who never spoke to her? It wasn't like that, it was not that sort of feeling. But one that she had not experienced before and therefore could not explain.

She decided that early in the morning she would go to the very extremes of the wood and watch to see which direction he came from. The following day she would try another boundary.

That night she woke abruptly, pulled from a deep sleep to instant awareness. For a moment she lay in the deep wide bed, wondering what had woken her. She rolled her head and saw the hands of the alarm clock making a green L in the dark beside her. Then she heard not far from her window the jingle of a bit, the stamp of a hoof. Quietly she rose from the bed and crept across to the vertical band of silver where the curtains met. Cautiously she opened them a fraction and looked down. Although she half-expected what she saw, it still came as a shock to see the horseman there. He was just below her window, his head level with her feet, gleaming like steel in the moonlight. He was looking straight at her. Slowly, as if impelled to do it, she drew back the curtains, half-aware of the sudden glow of the moonlight on her long cotton night-dress. He did not take his eyes from her face. At first she was trembling, but his stillness seemed to infect a stillness back in her, and she remained there, barely breathing. Quite casually the horse stretched out its head to just below her, tore some old leaves off the wistaria and munched them.

She turned and ran then, as fast as she could, down the stairs, across the hall, out of the front-door. But he was gone. She stood on the weedy gravel, unable to believe it. Then she ran down the path to the woods, bare feet in the wet mushy leaves, cold air passing icily through the thin gown. She called, begging him to return, not to leave her again, pausing every now and then to listen. She hurried on, able to see the path in the moonlight. Then she froze. The sounds were coming from behind her; the sounds of a man weeping. She held onto the bark of a tree to steady herself. The sounds seemed to rend the ground, make it tremble, shake the tree itself. She saw him riding towards her, slowly, with slack reins, head bowed, his sobbing like the blows of an axe, the rending of the wood it severed, and the shaking of the ground it struck. He loomed over her, a huge dark shape, and a stirrup brushed her arm, one of the horse's hooves clipped a stone. Appalled, she watched him continue down the path, disappear into the depths of the woods. There was nothing she could have said, have done, nothing even that she could think. There was an icy, empty stillness all around her. Shivering, she ran back to the house.

It was strange to turn on switches, have lights restore rooms to familiar dimensions, see all the ordinary accoutrements of her existence around her as if there to reassure her. She put on a sweater and went into the kitchen to make a cup of coffee. Although it was impossible to project the image of the moonlit horseman against the warm light and domesticity of the kitchen, the saucepans, kettle, spice-jars, sink and cupboards, she could still feel him there before her eyes like some invisible framework attached to her retinas. But her mind seemed to be able to make no sense of it, it seemed struck with a degree of paralysis. When she thought that she could have helped him in some way, even grabbed his reins as he passed and led him back to the house, tried to make him explain, she felt no regrets, only a kind of shocked numbness at something she could not comprehend. But she still determined that the next morning she would rise early and go to the far end of the wood to see what direction he might come from.

The route she took led across the hill from which it was possible to view the church. It particularly caught her eye that morning as the last leaves had fallen from the intervening trees and it stood out like a cleaned painting, even though the early sunlight had not yet pushed back all the mist. But there was something familiar in the graveyard. The sight made her heart jumped. Half-masked by one of the grassy mounds, was the figure of the horseman. Immediately she changed direction, breaking into a run, heading for the church. She did not stop to think, her only anxiety was to see him again. Once she was down from the hill, the church was lost from view till at last she reached the road, breathless now, from her haste. She ran in through the old iron gates, past the church, in among the polished black and white headstones and the bowls of faded flowers, looking round the mounds for a sign of the horseman. But he was no longer there. She ran to the chest-high stone wall to look out across the fields, to listen. But there was nothing. She thought he must have ridden up through the village. As she turned to retrace her steps, she paused at where she thought she had seen him standing. It was the old corner of the graveyard, beside the ruined walls and their crests of ivy. The gravestones here were old, most had either fallen, sunk into the ground or tilted over at grotesque angles, and all had long since lost their inscriptions. Except for one, that stood apart from the rest. She crossed the long wet grass to read it. Just the christian name was left, quite clear. ANNE-MARIE.

All she saw was the dark inscription in the grey lichen-crusted stone. Her surroundings vanished, her head pulsed with a deafening rhythm, there was a rushing sound as if a great wave of water were pouring towards her. Her vision melted, the letters wrinkled, distorted, broke up into fragments. And she lost consciousness.

When she opened her eyes she was lying on a sofa in a strange room. It was absolutely quiet except for the whispering tick of a clock, meticulous and peaceful. Above her hung a three-branched chandelier of metal with pink glass shades. There were heavy plaster cornices along the tops of the walls, which had a faded olive-green paper and were hung with mezzotints and engravings of romantic landscapes in pale walnut frames. She seemed to have all the time in the world to become aware of this room. It was like an isolated Victorian decompression-chamber. Over the marble fireplace was a mahogany overmantel of small shelves held up by miniature pillars, inlaid with small china medallions and triangles of mirror. The shelves held porcelain ornaments and photographs in silver frames. Near the door hung a sacred heart. There was a television covered with an antimacassar. There were bookshelves and more books stacked on tables, others lay on the arms of chairs. There was the smell of pipe-tobacco, and something that might be French-polish. She felt utterly becalmed, almost mindless, as if she were lying there like a baby of a few weeks.

It could have been hours later, or merely a few minutes later, when the door opened. Two women came in, followed by a man whose skin was as clean as a freshly peeled apple, so that she knew instinctively he must be the doctor. Behind him came the priest, a pair of reading-glasses on the end of his nose.

She could not explain what had happened to her, so she let them assume that she had simply fainted. The two women were sisters who acted as the priest's housekeepers. Everyone was full of concern, but she insisted there was nothing the matter with her and placated the doctor by agreeing to call at his surgery the following day for a check-up. The priest insisted in turn that he would drive her home later in his little-used car. After the doctor had left, and his housekeepers had gone to make her some tea, the priest said he wanted a word with her, and sat down, taking off his spectacles to clean them with a handkerchief before putting them into a pocket-case.

He told her that he knew her name was Anne-Marie. The Anne-Marie on the headstone had died over a hundred years ago. Her body had been found floating in the large lake. There were bruises on her head as if she had been kicked by a horse. But the cause of the accident was never discovered. Her husband had lost his reason as a result, and would ride through the woods, day after day, calling her name. Some of the villagers knew of people who had seen him, still riding through the woods, though he had died in an asylum only a year after his wife's death.

Anne-Marie had sat very still, listening intently. It could have surprised her, horrified her, scared her even. But instead of commenting, she told the priest something in return. She told him what her city doctor had told her to forget. It was so easy to tell, so prosaic now, nothing traumatic about it anymore. The tiny child she had accidentally killed with her car. A happy, pretty little girl she knew well, often waved and smiled at in the street, often talked to. So why had she to be the murderous instrument of such an unnecessary death?

She felt glad she had told the priest, smiling at him for his sympathy, as she brushed tears from her eyes. She felt as if a great weight had been removed.

Back in the house she began to wish that Henry would return. For the first time she felt lonely. She wandered through the rooms, stared out of the windows. A soft gold light coloured the topmost tree branches where they rose clear from the smoky evening mist. On the far side of the lawn blackbirds were busy tossing the wet copper leaves aside.

Conception

They had just turned off the television set and the coffee they were drinking was almost cold.

—Wouldn't it be awful not to have a past? the woman said. She was young, with thick dark hair. Those kingfisher days before we were married.

—You were thin as a child, the man replied.

—We didn't have to think about the problems of living then, she said. We just lived. The piano would jumble as if it had a speech impediment, she began to rhapsodize. While we scissored our bodies about the boards, and pumped ourselves up on the bar till we'd enough India-rubber in our bones to bounce to the moon. In the break there'd be coffee mugs hot as blushing faces between our hands, and under the table our throbbing legs cooling together. We were a flock of acrobatic swallows, woollen tights about our legs, vests for our chests. When the night came we painted out our faces to become the creatures we'd been practising to be, and whirled above the wax bright lights. To think I could control my body then as I can flex my fingers now, she added. It was really living.

—Those were the days, he said with a laugh, and not to be outdone, began to rhapsodize in his turn. All those prime white canvases waiting for one to squash paint over them like kids splashing through puddles. Our eyes were like flies crawling across the pink slabs of a woman motionless as a fish on a marble counter. Till she came to life, slipped on a gown and left her image repeated on twenty sheets of paper. Sometimes we ate the day like a swarm of locusts, drank coffee from an hour-glass, sat on the grass and talked the sun across the sky with headless intellect. And crab-like teachers would come and poke cold fingers of hindsight and impinge their boring well-thumbed images upon your own, while you itched to smear their faces with vermilion and carry on your own misbegotten way. I really felt alive then, he added. Give me any idea and I could make something of it. Now we're like trees tied to the ground by their roots.

—Stuck in the mud, she agreed. Not for much longer, though. It can't go on like this. Come on, let's go to bed. The sunshine in the morning is our only pick-me-up. I'll go and shut up the ducks.

She took a torch and went out. He collected the supper tray, took it to the kitchen and began to wash up.

When he had nearly finished he began to feel annoyed that his wife hadn't returned to help him. He folded away the cloth and went out of the back door thinking of a suitable sarcasm. The yard light was on and he walked across the gravel towards the duck sheds.

The ducks were always quacking in their didactic fashion, but it only struck him halfway across the yard that it was unusual at such a late hour. Suddenly he heard the sound of running. He stopped, surprised. Then he saw two young men in leather jackets running hard towards the gate.

—Stop them, stop them, he heard his wife's voice calling.

He hesitated for a moment, having no wish to run after their receding footsteps into total darkness. The obvious answer was to follow them in the car so that he could use its headlamps to see them. He got in quickly, revving the engine noisily, the roar giving him encouragement so that he raced out through the gate, the wheels scattering gravel, the lights seeming to set the trees and hedges on fire as they swung through them. He accelerated fast down the avenue and there they were, small white figures running ahead of him.

Just as they reached the gates he saw there was a car parked outside. He skidded to a halt and leaped out as they scrambled, cursing and breathless, into it. Before he could reach the nearest door, they roared away, racing through the gears like yelping dogs. He tore back to his own car and took off after them, his foot flat on the floor. Theirs was only an old banger and he soon caught up with their dim tail-lamps.

He was barely twenty feet behind them as they came into the sharp left-hand bend. The car in front slewed over to the far side, leaning as it tried too late to turn. He had no option but to sweep past on the inside, and in the instant the sky went wild with spewing light. The sound of bursting metal was like a church-organ bursting in mid-fugue. He glimpsed in his rear-view mirror a kind of monstrous skull with flapping ears rolling after him, shrieking and exuding flashes of light. When it dropped behind he stopped and looked back. It was as dark and quiet as if nothing had happened. He turned the car in a gateway and drove back cautiously to the bend, half-afraid that the two men might still leap out at him. But everything was all over the road, carseats, wheels, pieces of metal, the car itself upside down, like a skeleton picked clean by vultures. Dark stains over the tarmac reeked of petrol. He didn't dare look closely at the two figures sprawled in the wreckage.

He heard a car coming behind him, saw the lights and ran to wave it down. It was a police car. What a coincidence, he thought, till he realised his wife must have phoned for them. They were very considerate, as if the two men had been his own relatives. He was shaking so much that one of the policemen had to drive him back.

His wife was waiting in the doorway with the wife of the man from the gatelodge. They sat him down with a glass of whiskey. Then she took the policeman down to show them the duck-sheds.

The whiskey relaxed him.

Later, after everyone had gone and the tension drained away, he began to laugh. It was mostly reaction, but partly the state of his wife. She was covered in muck, her clothing all smeared and smelly, and she had wiped some of the filth off onto her face.

—Very funny, she said, avoiding his eyes. I hid when I first heard noises. But they saw me. When they heard you coming they shoved me in the muck and ran for it. Poor bastards, she added.

—Come on, he said. You need a bath.

—Didn't you wonder what happened to me? she asked, turning at the foot of the stairs. You never came out to find me. They might have killed me.

—I didn't know anyone was there. Anyway I heard you shouting at me to stop them.

—It could have been my last cry, couldn't it? she retorted, as if hoping to create discomfort to gloat over.

—Hardly. He shook his head. God, I'm tired, he complained.

He noticed as she went ahead up the stairs the muck was even up the backs of her thighs.

In the bathroom he sat on the windowsill and watched her cellulosing herself with soap, the soft pink plastic shapes dribbling with bubbles. He wanted to forget what had happened. He tried to remember what they had been talking about before, to introduce a distraction.

—The past, he said. We were talking about our pasts.

He could feel his words sounding artificial, half impeded by steam, half picking up the iron echo of the bath.

She was silent, as if debating whether to return to the topic.

—Our children will have a past the moment they're baptised, she said.

—What do you mean by that? he asked. Anyway I don't think we ought to baptise them. We should let them make up their own minds when they're old enough.

—But we must, she said, her sponge half-squeezed against her breasts, dribbling suds between them. We can't bring them into the world without something to hold onto.

—They'll have us, he replied. Why should we insist to them there is a God. I'm determined never to tell lies to my children. Never.

—But aren't we going to bring them up as Christians? she asked. It's still the foundation of modern civilisation.

—It makes no allowance for the development of a rational mind, he replied. I want my children to understand what they do and why.

His wife frowned, moving the sponge about her body automatically.

—Come on, he said. I want a bath, too.

—I always thought you believed there was a God of some kind, she said, a little incredulous, more at this unknown facet of her husband than the fact itself.

He shrugged.

—I used to hope there was, he replied.

She washed herself underneath, remembering the two dead men again. Washing away what had happened to her.

—I still think, she said, that they need God to believe in as children. Even if it is only a fairy story. Chuck me a towel, she added, pulling out the plug. However honest and frank you are with our children, she said, wrapping the towel round her body, as if now that it was clean, what had happened to it needed to be hidden from him, they'll come up against all the other beliefs that other children have had from their parents when they mix with them at school. The teachers will tell them different things from you.

—I know, he replied, undressing. But if a child is brought up to see for itself there are different sides to every point of view then he should be better able to tolerate their prejudices.

He turned on the taps, flooding fresh clean water into the bath.

—A kid's a kid, she said. You'll make it all too complicated. They'll end up so muddled they'll become neurotic.

He laughed, nudging her towel-clad form out of the way.

—If they ask, I shall answer. If they're in trouble, I'm on their side. There won't be any lectures.

—All this talk, she said, patting powder over herself. We haven't got one child yet. And a sudden panic fled through her body like a douche of cold weater.

They lay in the crisp bedsheets side by side, listening to the radio.

—I feel exceptionally clean, he said.

—Cleansed of tonight? she asked. Like Pontius Pilate?

—I don't think I'm that callous, he replied. I never even saw their faces.

His wife shivered by his side.

—If I hadn't chased them, they'd still be alive, he said.

—They'd still be alive, she whispered, if I'd shut the ducks up earlier.

—Don't let's think about it, he said.

—Do you ever remember when you were at school? he asked a little later. He looked at her with her eyes shut and a pained expression round her mouth. You did go to school, didn't you? he asked, mockingly.

—I don't like thinking about that either, she said.

—It used to be so simple at school, he mused. You soon understood the rules that governed your life. If you didn't get up when the bell rang, you didn't get any breakfast. If you didn't do your work you had to stay in when everyone else was free to enjoy themselves. You may have disagreed with many of the things that had to be done, but it made life easier to do them. Only one always had the impression that because it was forbidden to do something, it wasn't necessarily wrong. It was only done to maintain the school pattern. So you left school stamped with this pattern, unable to adapt to any other, unable to mix with anyone else except the same type-cast males, knowing nothing whatever about women except that the ultimate object was to get them on their backs. Yet it seemed all right when we were there. It was even better when we were prefects. We lived like executives with small, pretty secretaries to make coffee, mend our socks and make our wet-dream-stained beds.

—What about when you were little squirts and got beaten every other day? asked his wife.

He laughed.

—It was accepted as part of the pattern. There were so few who were gentle. As if teaching has to be like the job of sergeant-major, only suitable for loud bullies.

—That's why I don't like to think back on it, she said. I prefer to remember escaping into the woods after lessons or pedalling my bicycle into the town for my ballet lessons. Riding on top of the hay when it was brought to the yard, talking to the men about their love lives, making them blush and chase me to tickle me. I suppose I remember Paris. Being dragged round the great stone battleships, the Louvre, Versailles, in between dancing classes. It was a greenhouse life, we were watered and cossetted like hothouse plants in case the dreaded frost or some weevil might get us. We read every magazine ever forbidden in the lavatories. But they only mystified us. I remember when a maid got pregnant it got round that she achieved it through rubbing bottoms with the delivery boy from the boulangerie.

She stopped, suddenly uncomfortable.

—It's odd, he said, not noticing. How neither of us ever seems to bring our parents into our memories. Yet they must have been dominant figures.

She laughed.

—Sometimes I think the only reason I got married was to get away from mine. They destroyed my chances of ever becoming a good dancer. We can't let you be so far away from us, they'd simper, meaning they'd cut off my allowance. They needed me as a buffer for their quarrelling. And as part of the happy family image, some shiny white paint to put over the rotting wood.

—You really hate your parents, don't you? he murmured.

—Not really, she replied. At times. When they were lying themselves stupid. Now they leave me cold.

He nodded.

—I often feel guilty at not feeling sorry enough when mine were killed. They just slipped out of my life as if they'd never existed. He propped his head on an elbow. We won't be like our parents, will we? We'll live for our children. He smiled to himself. I used to dream of being a father. Even at school. Of loving my children. Showing it all the time. Trying to atone for my parents, I suppose.

His wife threw back her head and laughed.

—You sound so pretentious, she exclaimed. I expect our parents lay in their beds one night and swore the same. But the worries of making ends meet and the tribulations of trying to get on with each other shortened their tempers till they soon forgot their vows.

He shook his head.

—You can laugh, he said. I know we won't be like that.

—How about the two boys who died tonight? she demanded. Where's your conscience about them?

—Why must you bring them up again? he complained, sitting up. It wasn't my fault. They shouldn't have come after our property. You could say it was their own guilt that killed them.

—You'll say it was the child's fault when you beat him for doing something that displeased you too, won't you? Don't worry, she went on before he could protest. I'll probably be the same. We all make promises with the inevitable hypocrisy that we meant well at the start.

—Is this why we've put off having a child for so long? he asked.

She sighed.

—You haven't talked like this for months, she said. Is it just because you're upset by tonight? Are you? You're sure we can't just pretend it was all a game, finished with now, the toys put back in the cupboard and us washed and clean in bed?

He looked at her steadily.

—Let's start a child now, he said.

She stared back at him, unable to prevent a flush of guilt spreading right through her body. She wanted to ask, why now? Why not wait longer? All the excuses like wanting to travel unencumbered are just as valid now, aren't they? But she didn't say any of it. She couldn't say anything.

—I don't know why we never did it before, he said. Perhaps we were too good at making excuses. Perhaps I'm realising my creative work is too stunted and that it's time to make something real.

She laughed. Then her tone changed.

—And what about me? she demanded. Women are involved in this sort of thing to some extent. She closed her eyes. Why are we arguing? she muttered. Why have we always argued? We complain about it being dull in the country and do nothing about it. Spend hours remembering the good old days because we can't see the future. We're moribund with talking. Like you mixing all your colours up into mud.

And instantly the memory of the duck-shed, like a Breughel painting of a brutal farmyard scene hanging in the background, came into sharp focus.

Lying in the muck, muddy hands pressing her down, not knowing exactly what to do with her, their hesitation building up in her a sudden crazed desire to be raped, so that as she struggled to get away she pulled them down on top of her, and they all became entangled in a fight of confused motives, slithering amongst the slimy stinks of the duck-shed floor, before they found themselves achieving what they hadn't expected, and she realised it was too late to prevent it. But in the end they had freed themselves, pushed her down and fled.

—Yes, she went on fiercely. An atonement. Tonight we'll make a life for the two that ended.

—I don't understand you, he said, as she pulled off her nightdress with what seemed to him to be crude bravado. What's it got to do with them?

The Last Sandcastle

The beach is a great plain of empty sand. It is soft and damp, riddled
with small transparent hoppers that emerge and bite like angry fleas.
Feet sink six inches at each step and leave trails of narrow craters after
one.

Behind the beach the dunes lie like petrified waves hairy with
grass, to the north some hazy blue hills jut out into the sea, to the
south a stone cairn at the end of a causeway marks the entrance to an
estuary. A man and a boy are walking out across the sand, their
tracks like meandering stitching.

David Ronan and his son Matty. The boy aged five is carrying a
large red bucket and a small metal spade. They are heading out to
reach the edge of the sea nearly half a mile away, the tide just on the
turn. Already small in the distance behind them four or five small
children build castles in the drier white sand under the watchful eyes
of their mothers sitting gossiping in the sedge-grass of the dunes. Far
away to their left are some specks that are people walking.
Otherwise the two are quite alone on this great flat expanse of the
world.

Matty, a bundle of wiry limbs, cannot contain his nervous energy
to trudge beside his father, and darts backwards and forwards,
laughing and giggling, sometimes down on all fours pretending to be
a dog. Both of them become fascinated by their tracks and start to
hop and prance about making different patterns as if to confuse
supposed followers into thinking they were on the trail of a human
kangaroo or a lurching dromedary or a one-legged ostrich. In this
fashion they progress towards the lip of the sea.

Along the waterline searching seabirds hurry away at their
approach, rolling along the glistening sand like tennis balls.
Occasional gulls vault on their wing-tips over the slippery waves.
Matty runs ahead. The sand has become firmer, ribbed by the
soundwaves of tidal rhythms.

Neither of them has any intention of bathing. David takes off his shoes and stands with water oozing among his toes, surveying their solitariness. In all directions the world stretches away in endless flatness, apparently deserted except for the gulls and oystercatchers, and a freighter anchored a mile out across the calm sea, waiting for the tide to allow it to cross the bar and enter the estuary. Matty has already begun to chop haphazardly into the wet sand with his spade.

They dig a river to bring water into a pool, make a small castle that Matty promptly jumps on and flattens. They build another that the tide swills over and smoothes away. David does most of the digging, but sometimes Matty snatches the spade to dig a hole himself. They are absorbed, digging and channelling, slowly retreating before the encroaching tide.

Some distance away a solitary pink man in bathing trunks jogs towards the sea, his arms swinging up to his chest in the manner of a long-distance runner. David is sweating from his exertions and pauses to watch, while Matty throws sand at some gulls. The man runs into the sea, slows down and wades out a long way before the level of the water even reaches his thighs.

From the other side two diminutive figures slowly increase in stature as they approach, assuming identity by their different gait, a man and a woman, diffident, elderly. David resumes his digging.

—Dig a well, Daddy, dig a deep, deep well, implores Matty.

But the sides keep falling in, and it becomes a pool with a soft oozy bottom. Matty stands in it and exclaims with satisfaction that he no longer has any feet. David tries to build pinnacles by letting wet sand dribble through his fingers. But Matty keeps washing them away with bucketfulls of water, shrieking with laughter.

The elderly couple pass behind them and stop to watch, smiling.

—You're so lucky, they say. Yes, very lucky to have all this lovely beach to yourselves.

They have clipped English accents, and nod with shy friendliness. David agrees, they comment on the good behaviour of the summer weather, nod again and pass on, walking in their slow fashion. The pink man has emerged from his swim and begun the long run back to the dunes.

By this time all previous efforts at castles and fortifications have been smoothed flat by the ever absorbing tide. David decides to erect a larger mound, starting some yards inshore, to see how long it will withstand the creeping waves.

To distract Matty's continual efforts to flatten his handiwork, he has to build small diversions, so that by the time he has the sandcastle built up two feet the thin spill of the waves is already lipping its base. Working quickly with the small spade has tired him and he pauses breathing heavily. He is constantly being made conscious of his condition at the age of forty. The slightest physical effort tires him. Too much sitting in his daily life, swinging steering-wheels, placating telephones, lecturing dictaphones. At home he has to discard his shirt when guiding the motor-mower over the lawns even on a chilly day, to avoid becoming drenched with sweat.

Matty scrambles up onto the mound of sand and exclaims that he is the king of the castle, then becomes nervous of climbing down and David has to lift him. Together they watch the ripples lick the foundations, eroding the submissive sand, and David has to restrain Matty from helping. The boy dashes off and starts digging a hole with his hands like a dog, sand flying out between his thin brown legs.

They are completely alone now, the empty flat plain of beach without sign of people. Above them the sky is coloured a thin beige, plumes of cloud washing away into hazy films of gold and cream. He cannot help marvelling at the sensation of spaciousness about them, emphasising their puniness yet somehow extolling their existence.

He determines to strengthen the sandcastle and picks up the spade again. The sand comes away in chunks but is so friable that most of it falls off the spade before it reaches its destination. So he has to dig faster, slicing and patting it down, but still enjoying himself.

The pain catches him under the arms swiftly and silently, like his own father lifting him from behind, surprising him as a child playing in the garden. It stiffens him with fright, petrifies him into a shrunken posture, the spade falling from his hands. The great plain of beach floats and tilts, rolls right round him in one long soundless revolution. He lies fallen on the hard wet sand as if turned to stone, the world around him still moving, terns wheeling, clouds unfolding like lace and dissolving, Matty digging again. The pain crushes him yet seems withheld one fraction of a second away. Words lie motionless in his throat, ready to speak, like loaded cartridges in a greased gun-barrel and he unable to reach the trigger. He is totally paralysed. Only his eyes record, like a camera still running after the tripod has collapsed onto its side.

Matty runs round him, lies down beside him in imitation as if imagining that his father is playing some strange sort of game. He giggles, gets up again and sits astride his prostrate father.

—Daddy, do some more digging. I'm going to tickle you.

His hands fly lightly about his father and he shrieks with laughter before suddenly deciding to do some more digging himself. David can feel nothing, not even frustration, nothing but a glassy paralysis, the pain stuck as if he were a block of wood into which someone had just embedded a heavy axe, wood and steel fused into one.

His head is lying on the side of the sandcastle as if it were a pillow, his back is to the sea.

—Daddy your clothes are getting wet, exclaims Matty. Quickly, get up.

He runs round, peering down in amazement. David imagines that he can feel the cold slicing of water as it swills beneath him as if the lower half of his now solidified body consists of some metallic substance.

—I'm going to lie down, too, says Matty, throwing himself down again beside his father. But he gets up quickly, nervous of the water.

—Stop lying there, Daddy. Don't lie there.

David can do nothing to reassure the boy. He finds that quite apart from being unable to move any muscle whatever, the whole concept of movement seems to have faded away. His mind still appears to function, but with an already accepted sense of isolation, aware that the mechanical systems have packed up, leaving him as if locked in a room high up in some deserted building, cemented to the floor, with nothing but a screen at one end on which a film is showing, the only thing still working, pictures with which he cannot communicate or affect in any way. It is almost like a film shot thirty years before of himself as a boy upon a beach. The film is dim, scratched and monochromatic with its beige sky and ochre sand.

The small wiry figure of Matty has abandoned all idea of digging and wanders anxiously about his father, his fingers in his mouth.

—Daddy, Daddy, he whines miserably.

David feels vaguely that if he could only summon enough strength, it might not exactly move him, but it might at least crack some sort of reassuring smile from his lips. But nothing, not even a quiver. It is nearly as ridiculous a situation as standing beside one's car at some deserted spot, having carefully managed to lock the keys inside.

He is aware that Matty is now some ten yards away being driven back by the tide, hovering uncertainly along the edge. The small waves dishing out to the boy's feet have already swilled over his legs, gently rocking him as they pass. The remains of the sandcastle are still protecting his head and shoulders.

It suddenly becomes quite clear to him, immutable as a few precise printed word upon a telegram. This is death. He cannot be saved. He is quite helpless, the beach is totally deserted, nobody can see him, and Matty is too young to understand and run to fetch help. He expects tears of self-pity to well into his eyes, but the ducts are empty, incapable. And besides, he feels no pity, nothing except a vague wish that he could somehow reassure his son, now nearly thirty yards away, a small disconsolate child slowly retreating before the incoming sea, sucking his fingers and whimpering. He wishes he could at least say Go home. Instead he has to listen to the continual crying of Daddy, Daddy, coming across the rustling of the waves.

The water is much higher now, near his face, the waves dragging at him as they pass. Drops splash over him, but he cannot feel them, only see them like someone inside a room watching rain smear the windows outside. He feels he must be cold, colder than he has ever been in his life, yet he cannot even register a shiver, so that the feeling becomes like a written note laid upon his desk.

The foreman at the works is always leaving notes upon his desk, never liking to speak to him face to face, waiting instead till he is out somewhere before slipping into his office to leave his complaint or suggestion on the writing-pad. His wife Margaret, with her fuzzy hair and pink cheeks and that slightly startled look, she leaves notes too, props them on the mantelpiece of the sitting-room, things like, Gone mushroom picking. Even he himself is forced to leave notes for her like, the Stars of Bethlehem need watering. And there's Matty leaving his meaningless scribbles lying about on the torn-out leaves of magazines. No, don't, he cries, when people try to clear them away, they're messages.

The images, smells, sentiments of his home lie strewn through his mind like a calm autumn afternoon. A sense of peaceful relaxation spreads unexpectedly through him. The windows outside are dim.

Then suddenly they go dark. He bursts with anguish, choking in stone fury. The sandcastle, the protecting mound has finally collapsed, and the waves drag him away, roll him face down into their wet air-exclusiveness.

Dusk is falling, the tide is halfway back across the half-mile stretch of the beach. Out in the darkening sea, across the bar, the freighter is showing her lights. The small boy alone on the vast expanse of sand, is sobbing, whining, not knowing what to do with himself, still wandering along the edge of the incoming tide, a tiny figure.

Behind the dunes on both sides of the estuary, houses are lighting up; windows glow orange, silver television screens in their depths. Cars have drawn up and parked outside the pubs in the village.

You Never Learn

—I was lucky to get away this evening, Laurie said. There's always a crowd in on Saturday night.

She reclined at her ease in the car, brown hair flowing down her green jumper, bared thighs symmetrical as a pair of cream vases.

They had stopped at a roadhouse a few miles from the town for a meal, and had now pulled off the road into a neglected lane.

The young man, Jimmy, leaned over to slip an arm round her.

—Not tonight Josephine, she said, pushing his hand away.

—What's wrong? he protested.

—I enjoy going out with you, she said. But do we always have to bring sex into it?

—Just when I'm feeling randy, he complained, sitting back in his seat.

—Is it all a woman's supposed to be for? she demanded. To be stuffed full of food and drink, solely to be taken down a back lane and screwed?

—I'm sorry, he protested. I thought you enjoyed it.

—I don't feel like it tonight. And it's not because I've got my period, she added. Or gone off you.

He took out a packet of cigarettes, offered her one and lit them. He looked down through the exhaled smoke at the evocative slit between the spread of her thighs.

—Do you keep it for someone special? he asked.

—Perhaps.

—Just my luck, he sighed. I should never have gone away.

He settled himself even further back into his seat.

—All right, he said. Tell me about this man.

—My boss.

—Your boss? But he's twice your age.

—I can't help that.

—What about his wife?

—He wants to leave her.

—Does she know?

Laurie shrugged.

—One suspects she might. She's a dreadful bitch.

—Perhaps you're just sorry for him?

—Maybe.

—God. Trust you to get involved in a situation like that. Will it come to anything?

—I don't know. He wants to give up the pub. Emigrate.

—And you'll go with him?

She nodded. She told him how over the months since she had gone to work at the pub she had gradually found herself attracted to the owner Harry Dillon, at first both of them being pushed together as allies against a common cause. His wife was one of those who, never able to accept their limitations, are thus consumed with a crazed and unachievable desire to prove themselves. She was ruthlessly amoral, always raiding the bar's tills, and manipulating everyone, even friends, in her efforts to achieve her ends. She had tried innumerable ventures, a caravan site, a launderette in the town, a hairdresser's, a wine bar, breeding mink, making rustic furniture, everything attempted unrealistically, all collapsing dismally. Harry stoically ran the pub, fending off his wife's creditors with one hand, while dishing out the beer with the other.

—He must have been nuts to marry the woman in the first place, commented Jimmy. But he must have something. He's got you at least. Everybody's got somebody.

—Now don't get maudlin, Jimmy, I know you, you're just obsessed with sex, why would you worry? You don't care about women as people. You can't talk cars or football with them. Honestly, you're only one stage up from dogs.

—That's just not true. I don't happen to know any women who don't chat a load of drivel. It makes one try to kiss them to keep their mouths shut. Except you, Laurie. You're different. But you don't realise how tempting you are, sitting there all made up and perfumed, looking alluring. I think you're just leading me on.

—You see? You can't put sex away for a second, can you?

He sighed.

—Doesn't he mind you coming out with me?

—I wish he minded more. He said it would be good for me. And that it would be a useful cover to stop his wife suspecting there might be anything between us.

They talked for another half-hour more, then Jimmy, still

chagrined, but at least sympathetic, dropped her back at the pub.

—I'm envious, thinking of you going back in there to him.

She smiled.

—When'll you be back in these parts? she asked.

—Not for a month or two. Maybe I'll look you up anyway. Just to find out what's happened to you.

—Thanks. And thanks for the meal, Jimmy.

She stood for a while on the empty tarmac of the forecourt, watching the red tail-lights recede, listening to the burble of the exhaust diminish. The night hung like a curtain around her. The bulk of the dark pub loomed behind like an enormous Victorian wardrobe. A few cottage lights glowed in misty isolation. She turned and went round to the back door to let herself in through the kitchen.

She was about to go upstairs to her room when she noticed a light showing under the sitting-room door. She knocked and opened it cautiously in case it should be his wife. But it was Harry, sitting on the edge of a chair.

—Were you waiting up for me? she asked, made tender by his distraught face, imagining that he might have been a little jealous.

He stared at her blankly, as if not comprehending her. He had pale skin, hollow cheeks and a drooping black moustache. His eyes usually had a nervous, bird-bright humour, but tonight they were as still and dulled as if nailed into his skull.

—What's wrong? she asked.

His lips worked silently for a moment, struggling to find sound.

—I've killed her.

A shiver ran up her spine.

—You've what? she gasped.

Again his lips worked silently for a moment, then a tiny light returned to his eyes.

—We had a quarrel, he said. In the bar after closing. It became a fight, and I clouted her over the head with a cider flagon. I must have smashed her skull. Not a breath out of her. He spoke tersely, as if trying to express it in de-hydrated, minimal form.

Laurie listened with gaping mouth.

—You fool, Harry. You fool, she whispered, and stiff with horror, she put her arms around him, kneeling to pull his head onto her shoulder. I was always afraid of something like this happening. You should have left her years ago.

—She was complaining about you going out, he said, speaking into the fibres of her jumper. She called you a lazy little slut. That's when I hit her.

—What'll we do now? she asked.

—Call the gardaí, I suppose, he said resignedly.

—Couldn't we do something else? she asked. Couldn't we bury her in the garden or dump the body in the sea? She deserved what she got, she was horrible. Why should you have to spend the rest of your life in jail because of her?

—She couldn't help being the sort of person she was, he said, shaking his head. I shouldn't have lost my temper. I pitied her. She was her own worst enemy.

—This is no time for pious remorse, said Laurie. She was a selfish cow. People were always saying they couldn't understand how you stuck her. Listen. Couldn't we say she's gone away ? She was talking of going to France to scrounge off her mother.

—But it'll make it seem like murder if we start telling lies. It was only a fight, I didn't mean to kill her. Maybe they won't be too hard on me.

—You're such a bloody fatalist, she cried, stamping her foot. This is our chance to be together. Don't you want that? There must be some way.

She went out, and he heard her going into the bar. A minute later she was back.

—I can't find her, she said. Did you say the fight was in the bar? There's lots of broken glass about. That's all I could see.

—Of course she's there, he exclaimed, pushing past her.

He turned on all the lights, stood for a moment staring down at the blue carpeting, at where he expected to see her. Then he began searching frantically, pushing tables and chairs out of the way, running in behind the bar, going into the outer bar.

—She's gone, he exclaimed, returning, wild-eyed. She was lying there. He pointed down at his feet. I'll swear she was dead. Her eyes were stuck wide open, like a wax dummy, and her mouth was full of blood.

—Obviously you were mistaken, said Laurie, her eyes wide with apprehension, as if expecting a bloody and revengeful figure to materialise from behind a door at any moment. You search upstairs and I'll look in the kitchen and the storerooms.

For a few minutes the whole building reverberated with the tread of feet and the banging of doors, as if they were purposefully making the noise to give themselves courage and intimidate any lurking unknown. They met in the hall, frowned and shook their heads at each other.

—I'll get the flashlight, he said. She could have crawled outside. We'll have to look everywhere.

They were quieter outside, listening, peering after the torch's beam, expecting at any moment that it would light up a body huddled on the ground. They looked in outhouses, sheds, into the car still in its garage. Not a sign.

—She must be somewhere, he exclaimed. It's ridiculous.

They went round the garden, shining the light everywhere, disturbed two cats eyeing each other under the rhubarb. They searched the car park, even went a little way along the road.

—She must be in the house, he said, and they hastened back. Did you look in the cloakrooms?

—No. Did you?

Back inside she searched his face, wondering if he could be making it up.

—How long ago did it happen?

—About an hour ago I should think. His face was ashen, fragile as the ash of burnt paper. His usually resigned brows were crushed together, he was chewing his lips.

Her instinct was to put her arms round him, hold him steady.

—Stop it, Harry. Let's search the house again, really thoroughly. Every press, all the cupboards. You do downstairs this time. And the cloakrooms.

They took some time over the search, both now certain they would find nothing, but having to be reassured like a nervous sleeper having to convince himself of the unlikelihood of there being anyone in the wardrobe before turning out the light.

—Let's have a drink, he said wearily, waiting for her at the foot of the stairs.

—I was thinking, she said, as he stood behind the bar, pouring out two brandies. She could have dragged herself out onto the road and thumbed a passing lift.

—But I'll swear she was dead.

—Obviously you were wrong.

—It was a hell of a blow. She went down like a tree. I put my ear to her chest. Absolute silence.

—You never did know which side the heart was on. Let's ring the hospital.

—You do it.

She dialled the number, while he stared at the receiver in her hand as if expecting some monstrous insect to leap from it. After a few questions she shook her head at him, and put the receiver down.

—No casualties since nine.

He frowned.

—If she'd been picked up by anyone, said Laurie, thoughtfully, you'd think the police would have been round here by now.

Harry came out from behind the bar, sank down into a chair, and stared blankly at the glass of brandy in his hands.

—Maybe that's what we're waiting for then, he said.

Laurie leaned on the bar as she had often done when there might be a lull in the orders and a corner of chat going on that she could join in. Except that now the place was empty, broken glass all over the floor, and her boss, Harry Dillon, was seated alone at a table, drinking brandy, something she'd never seen him do before.

—It's almost as if she planned it, isn't it? she suggested. Goading you into hitting her, pretending to be dead, getting us into a state of nerves.

Abruptly Harry got up and went over to the phone.

—What are you going to do? exclaimed Laurie.

—Ring the gardaí.

—Don't, she cried, gripping his arm.

He brushed her hand off.

—I must know, he said, dialling, then listening to the drawn-out ringing. Maybe they're closed for the night, he muttered.

—Look, she said. Don't give anything away. If she was going to them, they'd be round here by now. She's up to some other game.

There was a click, a voice.

—This is Harry Dillon, Harry spoke rapidly. Malone's Bar. You haven't seen my wife, have you? No, it's just that I can't find her. Nothing? No reports of any accidents? Car accidents? All right. I'll wait and see then. Goodnight, now.

—What did they say?

—Maybe she's spending the night with neighbours. They must be able to smell husband-and-wife quarrels a mile off. They get them all the time, I suppose.

—What are we going to do?

—What can we do?

—Just wait, said Laurie, slowly.

Harry lifted his gaze out of his glass and looked directly at Laurie. The first time that he had looked straight at her since her return. Then he sighed.

—These could be our last hours together, he said. The wheels have already been set in motion. And there's nothing we can do to stop them.

—I hate your bloody fatalism, she said. Maybe nothing at all will happen.

—Don't forget I all but killed her. Don't forget that.

—I think we should go to bed. We can't do anything. And if anything was going to happen, it would have happened by now.

—She's out there somewhere, he muttered, drinking down the last dregs of his brandy. We can't even sleep together.

—Of course we can, she said. Lock all the doors.

—I'd feel her looking over my shoulder, her presence hovering round.

—Don't be daft, exclaimed Laurie, automatically rinsing out the glasses.

—I couldn't, he repeated.

—Have it your own way, she muttered, following him up the stairs.

But later in the night he came into her room in his yellow pyjamas, slipped into bed beside her warmth.

—I was scared, he whispered. I could feel her watching me. I've got a terrible headache. Pains in my sinus.

Laurie made him drink some disprin, then turned out the light again. They lay listening to the depthless silence of the night outside, to the odd click of a waterpipe, creak of a floorboard, hiss of leaves outside. Then, when the silence really felt quite empty and safe, they made love, and fell asleep till woken by the clanging of an early morning delivery of beer kegs.

They spent that day with ears tuned to the utmost pitch, dreading after the sound of every car arriving to hear his wife's voice or the gardaí. They agonised each time the phone rang. Every window they passed, they stopped to look through. They were afraid to go out. Some shopping was needed, but neither wished to go into town alone and leave the other on his own, so they rang up and arranged with someone to deliver it in the evening. They tried to sound cheerful when serving in the bars, watching people's expressions for odd looks in their direction.

But nothing happened. Nobody mentioned her. Nobody came looking for her. Not a garda in sight. During the afternoon, Harry put on his gumboots and searched the fields and ditches all round the back of the yard. It was as if his wife had completely dissolved out of space and time. Her coats still hung in the cloakroom, her cigarette-lighter stood on the mantelpiece in the sitting-room, her bedroom remained pungent with her perfume and, most alarming of all, her handbag stood open on the kitchen table. Laurie put it upstairs in the bedroom.

Yet after the bar closed that night and they had finished clearing up, they couldn't help smiling at each other with relief. To have got through the day, both constantly tense with anticipation of imminent disaster seemed to suggest that theyw ere almost safe, that if she hadn't turned up by nbow, she had vanished for ever.

To embellish their new sensation of freedom they kissed and fondled playfully, as they had done rarely before, only on the occasions when his wife had gone to Dublin or been away hunting.

—I do love you, said Laurie, the palms of her hands cupping his face, his moustache ticking her nose.

—I'm a killer, you know, he said. Even if she is still alive.

—Don't talk about her anymore, she said. Let's just live for the present. It's marvellous to feel so free.

—We must be careful all the same, he said, and his eyes flicked sideways as if someone might be peering in through a window.

Upstairs they wandered about half-naked in and out of each other's bedroom and the bathroom, tickling and chasing each other so that the whole process of undressing and washing was prolonged with much spilling of water and collapsing in fits of laughter. They lay peeled on top of Laurie's bed, and abandoned themselves to love-making.

—I'd forgotten, Harry said at some later stage, lifting himself up like a freshly gnawed wishbone, how free it's possible to feel.

—Poor Harry, she murmured, smiling dreamily.

They fell into a deep hibernating sleep, limbs intermingled like trusting children.

The next day was dark, with windy rain rattling and splashing the windows. The bar remained practically deserted except for a crowd of disappointed golfers who drank a firkin of stout between them before leaving in the middle of the afternoon. The dampness of the day set a paralysing seal upon Harry. He stood in front of a window looking out across the water-streaked road, at bedraggled trees, and a group of cattle standing beneath them, their coats made glossy from the soak of the rain. Laurie came and put her arms inside his jacket, laying her head on his shoulder.

—You haven't had any lunch, she said. Would you like some cold beef or shall I make an omelette?

He put his hands over hers.

—She's plotting something, he muttered. It wouldn't be like her not to.

—Forget her, sighed Laurie. Wait till something happens. Maybe we'll never hear of her again.

—That's being stupid, he snapped. We should be trying to anticipate her next move. What can she be up to?

—It's not being stupid, she said sulkily. It's just that there's nothing to be gained by worrying.

She left him to his gazing and went up to her room, lay down on her bed and gnawed tearfully at her fingernails. She hoped he'd come up. But she heard him down in the kitchen, cooking himself something, so she went back downstairs.

—I'll do it, she said, annoyed, taking the pan out of his hands.

—What are you so grumpy for? he asked.

—You're not the only person here, she said.

He sat down slowly, gazed at his hands.

—The tension's still there. We can't stop it.

—I suppose so, she muttered.

—I wish something would happen, she said while they ate.

Two people had rung up during the day, and Laurie had replied that Harry's wife was away, without committing herself to any details. Then during the afternoon some friends rang up to ask Harry and his wife out to a party.

—What are we going to tell people? asked Laurie. We must have a consistent plan.

—We could give the partial truth, just say she's disappeared, walked out one night after a row, and nobody's seen her since.

—People'll start getting curious then, asking all sorts of questions. They'd want to know if we told the police. We can't use the truth, Harry, don't you understand?

He was patient.

—If we say she's gone to stay with her mother in France, people are going to think it odd when she doesn't come back, doesn't send anyone a postcard.

—But she did say a few days ago that she'd thought of going, didn't she? Wanted to get away from the poisonous atmosphere of the place. I heard her.

—We'll say that then, he said.

The days passed, and though a few bills came addressed to his wife, no letter came that might have suggested what had become of her. People in the bar asked after her, a man she owed money to came looking for her. Harry went to the party on his own. Then a letter came from France for her, in her mother's handwriting.

The postman was a nosy gossip, they knew he was likely to comment to the locals, probably when he was drinking in their own bar that very night. Harry was shaking, looking at everyone with suspicion.

—You look ill, Laurie whispered to him. I'll manage. You go and lie down.

But he refused.

—I must know.

When someone asked casually if his wife was still in France he practically shouted out the affirmative.

—You're so jumpy, murmured Laurie. What does it matter? You haven't done anything. Except for your fight, which anyone might have had.

Harry screwed up his eyes.

—Don't mention it, he snapped. Somebody might hear. Or they'll see us whispering and think it suspicious.

By the time the bar closed he was holding his chest and breathing hard.

—I'd like to sell the place in the morning and leave in the afternoon, he said. I can't stand this.

—That would look incredibly suspicious. We've got to sit tight.

He sighed.

—But it can't go on like this. He poured out half a tumbler of brandy each. I wish to hell I knew what she's up to.

He suddenly pointed at a long piece of cigarette ash that had burned itself out on a shelf.

—For God's sake, he snapped. You're as bad as she was. You'll have the place in flames.

—I'm sorry, said Laurie, her eyes narrowing.

When she was undressing that night he came into her room carrying a blouse, a pair of knickers and a pair of tights.

—Must you leave your clothes lying about the bathroom floor? he complained. It was bad enough with her doing it all the time.

—Don't accuse me of doing things that she did, cried Laurie, tight-lipped.

He looked at her hard, and their twin angers fused for a moment.

—Don't . . . he began, then took a deep breath. I'm sorry, he said, his voice softening. I don't know what I'm saying. It's the situation.

Her face was hard and she withdrew from his outstretched arms. But he closed up on her, encircled her shoulders, pulled her head against his chest.

—I'm sorry, he whispered.

She relented.

—I shouldn't be so touchy, she murmured.

They held each other crushed together as if trying to convince themselves that their divergent bodies could be united into one.

The next day was blustery, blazes of sunshine followed by swirls of cloudiness. The sort of day when nature seems intent on demonstrating its power, that it still has context in the modern world, encouraging one to marvel at its strength as the monstrous canyons of sky crash out of the heavens. It heeled like a sturdy boat, every blade of grass and branch of tree streaming in the wind.

—What I hate about a pub, said Harry moodily, as they stood out in the garden, letting the wind blow through their hair, ripple their clothes, is that it pins one down. Seven days a week.

—Ever since I've known you, you've said you wanted to sell it, said Laurie. I could never understand why you stayed on. You're not the type.

—I like the views, the landscape, being near the sea, and it's difficult to break a habit. I'd like to go for a walk today, he added, nodding towards the distant hills, blotchy with cloud shadow. Just you and I. Then we might really feel free from her watching eyes.

The bar was full of tourists that day and kept them busy. The next day he was angry because there was no lunch.

—I'm sorry, said Laurie. I just didn't seem to have time.

—You're as bad as her, he complained. She was always chatting for hours to people and forgetting all about meals.

Laurie froze.

—I can't take any more, she cried.

She ran out of the kitchen, leaving him holding a piece of buttered bread before his open mouth. He found her in the bedroom, throwing clothes into her cases, angry and red-eyed, hair falling down over her eyes.

—Don't be silly, he said. I didn't mean anything.

—I've got to go, she said.

—Please, he implored, coming round the bed to put his arms round her. I'm sorry.

She shook herself free.

—Why do you have to go on and on? she complained. You're not really interested in people, you just want things to be right. Maybe that's what was wrong with her. Driven to do stupid things because she could never get through to you, because you never wanted her, all you wanted was to get your little pattern of life right. So you drove her out of her mind. Now you want to start on me.

His mouth drew down and he glared at her.

—You know that isn't true, he said thickly. You're cracking up under the strain. That's all it is. It's as if she planned the whole thing deliberately, knowing that we wouldn't be able to stand not knowing what had happened to her.

—Why did you have to go and beat her up that night? cried Laurie, still continuing with her packing.

—Don't go, he said. How will I manage on my own?

—Is that all you think of? The bloody pub?

—It's the machinery of existence, he sighed. It's the same for all of us. He sat down on the bed. I don't seem to know you anymore. I feel as if all my files and daily records have been ransacked. Nothing left to identify the daily problem with. It doesn't seem to be you wanting to leave me. But someone else. I can't think what happened to you.

—It's no good, Harry, going on like that.

She leant on the washbasin, looking down into its bowl, her back to him.

—I don't want to leave, she murmured.

He put his arms round her and drew her down onto the bed, holding her tightly, kissing her wet eyes.

—Ohhh, she growled half-angrily from smothered lips. Why am I letting you do this to me?

He pushed the filled suitcase aside, and with the weather breezing through the open window, cars passing outside, and customers waiting downstairs in the bar, they made love; a sudden anguished manipulation of clumsy crucibles to catch the livid flow forcing its way through them. Then a bell rang, and they sundered in a manner that stuck with them for the rest of the day, cracked like buildings in an earthquake, that engineers cannot make their minds up about, whether to repair or to dismantle.

Sometime during the busy part of the evening, he commented about a yellow sweater she was wearing, that she was as bad at choosing clothes as . . . and he quickly swallowed the name, trying to laugh it off as if he had only been joking while she shrugged resignedly.

They were constrained while washing and undressing for bed.

—It's four days now, he said, sitting on the bed to pull off his socks. What on earth can she be up to.

—It feels more like a year.

—We're getting too complacent, he said. Living as if she's gone, and that's it. She must be dead. The silence doesn't make sense. She's not the sort of person to miss out on a chance to gain something over me.

—Or likely to give me the chance of gaining something over you, muttered Laurie.

In the bed, he brushed his fingers up and down the soft flank of her hips and she squirmed ticklishly.

—She used to do the same, he said sleepily.

While he slept, she wept.

At the first sign of dawn she slipped out of the bed and dressed, took her suitcase out onto the landing, put the last few bits and pieces in, then crept downstairs and let herself out of the house.

Without her presence to wake him, he slept late, then had to hurry to have the bars ready for Sunday morning trade, his reactions to her absence numbed by the needs of the pub. Without her to help him he was nearly run off his feet. When closing time came, he cleared up and fell asleep sitting on a chair in the kitchen while waiting for some soup he had made from a packet to cool.

The next day was a bank holiday and he was swept up by the rush for drinks, unshaven and half-asleep, quite unable even to begin to contemplate his position. The pub was like some infernal machine that he was trapped inside and forced to keep going. The demand was insatiable, he was never allowed to stop for a moment. If there was a lull he had to rush to replenish stocks, bring up crates or kegs. The two bars echoed with a thick intensity of chattering voices, but to Harry they roared like furnaces, and he was the stoker rushing backwards and forwards, gushing out the oily beakers of fuel to keep them going. The drawer of the till slammed in and out, becoming stuffed with notes like a box of cabbage leaves.

—Working hard today, Harry, commented someone. Got rid of both your women then? Did you bury them in the garden or the cellar?

Much laughter, effluence of froth dribbling down the fat wet sides of the stout glasses, more head scooped off to allow more black liquid in. Harry grunted monosyllabically, hurrying from one bar to the other.

After consuming a can of beans, he crawled to his bed that night, leaving the table in the kitchen littered with half-drunk cups of coffee, and bits of food he had begun to eat and been forced to abandon.

The next day had been taken as a holiday by many organisations, and the bar was again crowded. In despair, he set to again, his body stiff with exhaustion.

—If only she'd come back, he kept muttering to himself, polishing glasses, finding there were no more drying cloths and resorting to tissues. I'll have to advertise for someone. It can't go on like this.

He barely spoke to anyone, just functioned like an automaton, responding dutifully to requests for rounds, sliding them onto the bar, retrieving empties, bringing the change. Had he made a single mistake, something in his brain might have exploded, thrown him completely out of gear. The whole process became a blur.

The next morning a beer truck arrived to deliver fresh supplies. The driver found doors wide open throughout the pub, but no one responded to his calls. There were half-buttered slices of bread curling on the kitchen table, cups of half-drunk coffee, plates covered with uneaten food. When a few locals came up for their morning jar, they found the same emptiness, the bar still littered from the previous night, the till wide open, still full of money. They searched the house, found the bedclothes all rumpled, pyjamas and other clothes strewn haphazardly round the rooms, but no sign of anyone. They helped themselves to beer, put the money by the till and waited.

—Like another bloody Marie Celeste, somebody said.

On the Top of a
White-Bearded Hill

There were birds below him, far below, tiny specks gliding over the almost motionless wrinkles of the sea. He was afraid, yet exhilarated by being up so high, on the edge of so steep a slope. The path was little more than a runnel of clay, mostly used by sheep, and he imagined one slip would send him rolling down through the ferns, crashing through the wires of the fence, and out over the cliff. Yet if only he could lean forward, extend his arms and swoop off like a bird. It seemed almost plausible at that moment.

The circle of the bay was completed on his left by a rocky promontory extending out into the sea, and it hung beneath him like a funnel at the bottom of which lay a little alcove of a beach, washed by thin waves paling in from the deeper turquoise waters. The sea down there seemed limpid, cool, attractive. He felt he must descend quickly down the little string paths, down the cliffs, and slake his body in that limpid blueness.

There was nobody else in sight.

No, she had said, you go, I don't feel like a walk. So he had trudged across the thick grass fields by himself towards the hump of the headland, not exactly sure of what he would find on the other side, and then was amazed at the view, the endless extent of the sea, the steep grey cliffs running north. Tourists didn't seem to come up here, preferring the little coves, the ports and hamlets with their pubs and concrete toilets, and cars jammed round a crowded, almondy beach.

I'm tired after yesterday, she said. I know you like walking. You go on your own. Yesterday finished me.

In one sense yesterday had been the opposite of today. He remembered it as all ascent, up to the top of a conical hill white with dead grass, thick with gorse and heather. They had passed various abandoned cottages, shacks of board, with rusty corrugated iron roofs, half-buried in rank hedges. They had peered through dusty windows at abandoned beds, worn-out gum-boots, battered kettles left on cookers, pictures crooked on the walls, newspapers strewn across floors. Perhaps the people just died, she had said. And nobody wanted to come and live up here anymore. People prefer cities. In one house there was an ancient Victorian paraffin heater worthy of a museum, a wooden torch with a lens like a crystal ball, and on a shelf a row of eight mouse-traps. In another house dozens of half-finished canvases leaned against the walls.

The hill itself was bare, untended, white as Tolstoy's beard. When he had said, puffing with the exertion of the climb, that he didn't think the crest ahead could be the top, she exclaimed that she would go no further if it weren't. But it was. A crumbled tumulus on a flat plateau of grass; and all around a flowing, undulating skirt of fields extending far into the blue, hillocky distance.

Tomb-robbers or archaeologists had half-flattened the tumulus, their efforts to extract its past had made it into nothing more than a comfortable basin of soft grass to recline in. This is a ceremonial place, he had said to her. We should make love here. And without more ado she had strewn her clothing all around, and sat waiting as women have done for millions of years, naked forces of soft round whiteness. As she waited a pair of noisy gadflies swept past, startling her, making her leap up anxiously and run off a few paces. He had laughed and said, people will see you, a strange white creature cavorting on the tomb of their ancestors. She had returned then, and they had laid cradled in the grass, beneath the hot, cloudless sky, while insects buzzed across their skins, swallows swooped over the heather and a solitary buzzard wheeled high above; and the whole of existence passed through their loins.

He didn't really mind her not coming, he thought, as he descended the worn pads of grass that provided crumbling stepping places on the steep path. The loneliness was almost stimulating.

Above him now, on the crest of the headland, were the half-hidden roofs and aerials of a coast-guard station. Below him jutted out the rocky promontory, the first half of it a cracked and shattered squeeze of petrified lava, partially covered with a sheep-shorn mantle of grass, and the second, almost an island, like a massive slab of layer cake slugged on its side in the sea, full of even lines of creamy marble filling. Ships must have been wrecked on that, he thought. Hundreds of years ago. On wild nights, men must have drowned down there, dashed against the crags. He stared in horrified fascination. Yet all was so still and serene now, the sky an empty void above, the sea like the glossy coat of a sleeping beast.

The mass of water was a deep turquoise, greying towards the horizon. Yes, his body thirsted to be inside it. He steadied himself as he descended, still afraid of falling.

At last the path levelled out and he crossed a small field to a gate that led onto the promontory. The gulls swinging over the bay were only just below him now, and he could see the hooked blades of their beaks and small bright eyes as they glided round.

It was as he began to descend the path to the little cove that he entered the aura of sea noise and for the first time became aware of the rinsing hiss of waves as they pushed and foamed mildly about the base of the cliffs.

The water had that rich appetising colouring of wine, even though it was blue and not red, and he imagined it already soft and cool about him. He was no longer afraid of falling now, even though the path was narrow and tight against the sheer rock of the cliff. As his feet trod at last on the taut, damp sand he was tense with excitement, and began quickly unbuttoning his jacket.

If she had known he was going to swim, he thought, watching the light waves reel in and fail to reach his feet, she would have come. But once in the water she would have swum about teasing him, diving down and grabbing his toes, scaring him; she was too good a swimmer for him. No, this was how he liked it, himself and the world, the sea and the cliffs, alone together. He thought to himself that he should at least have brought a towel. But he was too greedy for the water. He piled his clothes on a rock and ran down naked into the shallows, wading out and throwing himself forward into the sudden cold engulfment of the sea.

For a few minutes he swam around lazily, feeling the sluicing bubbles passing all the way down his body, searching and rinsing every crevice like the waves drenching the cracks in the rocks all around. Then he swam back and lay in the shallows, letting the waves rock his body as they swilled over it. He was at the bottom of a funnel, he thought, looking round. The cliffs towered steeply upwards, immense slate walls encircling him. Only across the bay, high above the mainland cliffs could he see any sign of life, bits of green field, trees and the roof of a house. He felt a little uneasy at his isolation.

A breeze flitted, crocodiling the water, chilling his shoulders, so he pushed himself down into deeper water and swam out slowly. He swam across to the nearest part of the promontory, found a rock he could climb onto and sat for a few minutes under its looming bluff. It was peculiar, he thought, how once out of the water, its blue colour became instantly appetising again, and he wanted to be back inside it. He would have liked to dive in, but felt nervous of so blatant a gesture in a situation that dominated him with mingled tensions of exhilaration and fear.

She would have laughed at him, he thought. Told him not to be such an idiot. Goaded him into doing it. He tried to visualize her back at the cottage, probably sprawled in a chair, reading a paperback, as calm and contented as a well-fed cat.

Human-beings were strange creatures, he thought, looking down at the hairs matted in herring-bone patterns all over his wet thighs. So white in colour, these shanky tubular limbs that stretch out in so many directions, or fold up into all sorts of positions, ugly really, beautiful only in moments of reflection, one posture in fifty that catches the eye. He remembered her as she ran from the gadflies on the hilltop, her flesh quivering as it clung to her bones, a big pink blotch on each buttock, and then as she turned on one foot a moment of grace that seemed to hang in his memory for eternity, as if it were the movement she had been running to make, a livid flowing form in slow revolving suspension on the top of a white-bearded hill.

He slipped back down into the water and swam slowly back towards the little strip of sand.

As he swam he suddenly thought of creatures in the deep, down below him, of how his body must dangle its white limbs temptingly above them, of how their sharp teeth and long tentacles might even now be reaching out for him. The sky had darkened, evening was falling. As he looked round he thought he could see dark shapes beneath the water, moving closer, swimming under him, and with stiff and desperate strokes he clove through the water, splashing wildly, choking and swallowing, struggling to reach the sand. His feet touched bottom and he hurled himself forward, gasping and coughing, till he was clear of the water. He stood with his back to the cliff and stared as if expecting to see the surface broken by fins, the swirling of great bodies, opening jaws. But there was nothing but a vague marbling of bubbles made by his hasty exodus. He began to regret his flight. He wanted to be back inside that water again, but was afraid now. He wished he had a towel to dry himself, and tried brushing the drops of water off himself by rubbing his hands down over his chest and legs.

How she would have laughed, he thought. Called him an idiot. But truth is too easy a stick to use. It cannot prevent those spectres haunting one out of those primæval distances of the past, as if instinct still nurtures memories of dinosaurs closing in hungrily.

He wondered if she ever felt fear in the same way, saw threats in shadows, heard menace in sounds, dreaded being left alone in a house at night. If he asked her, she would probably just laugh, close up and bite him playfully. Come to think of it, he supposed she constituted some kind of threat as well. There was a degree of menace in everyone, everything.

Dusk was falling and he hurried to put his clothes on. They were reluctant to slide up his damp limbs and he cursed as he ripped a button from his shirt. Feeling sticky and awkward he began the climb up from the little cove. The water had gone the colour of pewter and was full of dark eddies swirling round the rocks. He was glad to be leaving. He leaned against the rockside of the cliff and eased himself up carefully, looking behind as if to check that nothing was following. He was considerably relieved when his head rose above the level of the promontory and he was able to view the geometric limit of the sea spreading across the horizon, the water paler than the sky, streaked with flat tones of pink and silver.

The great block of the headland loomed darkly over him. He still had to get round that, to reach the far side, and descend to the village where he had arranged to meet her in the pub. It was difficult to distinguish exactly where the path lay, and he cursed himself for not having started earlier. He began to follow it cautiously, climbing at a steep angle over the safety of the field that led out to the promontory. But when the path levelled out, he looked down and noticed that it was now directly over the cliffs again, and he could see white foam circling the rocks beneath. It seemed to have become dark extraordinarily quickly.

He moved gingerly, holding onto the fern-sprouting rocks beside him, even though the path seemed quite wide. He could see lights clustering along the coastline in the distance, and wished he had a torch. It was lying on a shelf in the kitchen, together with a thermos flask and an aerosol fly-spray. He had put it there last night after coming back from the privy. But it was no good wishing for it now, after all, he had never anticipated being out so late anyway. She would probably be sitting in the pub by now, looking at her watch, sipping a glass of beer, cursing him for being late.

O well, he thought resignedly. He must be nearly round the headland by now, and soon he ought to be able to see the lights of the village somewhere below.

At some unthinking moment in the blind darkness he must have thought the path continued on where in fact it veered to the left. One minute he was on the path, the next his right foot descended into nothing and he was toppling face forward into ferns, clutching futilely at them as he rolled rapidly downwards and hit the fence with a clash of wires. Frantically he grasped at them, feeling his body slip through, and then as if it were done deliberately to horrify him, he felt himself hanging out over nothing, arms yanked upwards, the thin wires biting into his clutching fingers, the fence posts groaning with strain, and down below him the sea churning noisily about the bases of the cliffs.

Help, he cried. Help, help.

Stupid, he thought. Nobody could hear him. He swung his legs and his knees banged into hard rock. Rock everywhere, rock below him waiting to smash him to pulp when he could hold onto the wires no longer. O God, if only there were someone to help him. Why hadn't she come on the walk? It would never have happened then. And even if it had, she would have been able to do something, give him a hand or gone for help. He couldn't hold on for much longer. He was done for. Unless he could do something.

He pulled and strained till his face touched the wire, and held himself locked there, feeling his muscles quivering, taut as ropes, sweat trickling down his neck. He was able to rest his elbows on some kind of ledge, which helped to take some of the strain off his fingers. But as he swung a leg out sideways to try and gain more purchase, the ledge crumbled and he dropped back to dangle in space, the wires all but cutting right through his fingers, the posts cracking ominously above him. He screamed with fear and vexation. As he began to strain to pull himself up the second time, he felt certain he would never have enough strength to do it a third time.

Keeping his weight on the wire, his face contorted with agony, he lifted his elbows over the edge and eased himself forward cautiously till he could feel his shoulders brushing the wire above and could push himself high enough to get a knee onto the ledge, levering himself up gingerly in case it should break off again. Then he lay resting, pressing himself against the steep slope, but still clutching the wire. He could feel his heart thumping the ground.

After a while he began to ease himself forward again, almost reluctant to let go of the wire, even when it was behind him, but having to in order to reach upwards cautiously, holding onto tufts of heather, the stems of ferns, anything to give him reassurance, terrified that he might slip backwards at any moment. But at last he felt the path and crawled onto its level of safety, and there he sat, pressing his back against the rocks, unwilling to go any further for the moment.

Christ, that was close, he thought. Very close. He could feel shivers and trembles running through various parts of his slumped body, as if confusion still reigned inside him after the panic. She would be sitting in the pub, he thought, wondering what had happened to him. Perhaps she would be anxious. After all, it had so nearly been fatal. Would she have organised a search party? Or just gone home? People flashing their torches down the cliffs, over the rocks, finding the stretched wires, but nothing else, as the sea would have taken his body away with it. He wondered how upset she would have been. He did not know exactly how close they were to each other. He had seen her shed tears at moments of insecurity. But this would have been a new experience for her, to stand beside the newly-dug grave and watch the last sight of the coffin that contained a man whose body had been united with hers upon the crest of a white-bearded hill only a few days previously. She would be full of regret, he was certain of that. For there was always promise in retrospect.

After a little longer he stood up, cautiously holding onto the steeply rising ground beside him. He walked leaning inwards to grasp rock or fern or whatever he could, shuffling his feet along to make sure they didn't venture out into space again.

After a while the path began to descend, and he could see the lights of houses that clustered down in the cove where the village lay. Silhouetted against the luminous glow on the horizon he could make out that the fence had risen up beside him now, as if to help him on, give him confidence. The path seemed wider, safer.

Then he could make out the houses in a square, lit by three or four streetlamps, cars parked side by side. He realised he was walking slowly not so much because of the dark, but because he was exhausted. Little tremors still shivered within the weakness of his muscles.

He tried to imagine her reaction when he told her. Perhaps she would laugh in disbelief. Then he would show her the lacerations on his hands and the state of his clothes.

Once he had reached the square, the glare of the streetlamps made him look at himself self-consciously. His shoes were scuffed, the knees of his trousers were filthy, bits of heather were caught in the zip of his jacket, smears of dirt all over it and a rent from one pocket. Instinctively he tried to brush off the dirt to smarten himself up before entering the pub. But his hands were so sore he stopped. Besides he was thirsty for a drink.

Old pewter mugs hung on the beams in the bar, and there were two large panelled alcoves, one of which contained a dartboard, and the other a fireplace with unlit logs on the hearth. Several men were drinking at the bar, middle-aged couples were seated at tables. There was no sign of her. Perhaps she had become fed-up with waiting and left. He went over to the bar and asked if a girl with long mahogany hair had been in. The barmaid shook her head.

He was about to ask for a drink when he remembered that she had his wallet. He felt in his pocket. Nothing but a twopenny piece. He asked the barmaid if she would mind him waiting, and she agreed disinterestedly.

He sat down at a free table, looked round at all the customers chatting among themselves, reminiscing and laughing, the barmaid polishing glasses. He wanted to announce to them that he had nearly died half an hour ago, all but fallen off the cliff, just managed to save himself after hanging out over the abyss, was only here by a hair's-breadth of luck. But he could sense how unreal his words would sound. It didn't seem to matter anymore. He unclenched his sore hands and looked at the redness and the cuts. He would just sit here and wait for her.

He could see her again as she turned on the dead-grass hilltop, a revolving outstretched figure of milk-white, hair flying, arms suspended, floating round in the hot sunshine, as the insects buzzed all around and the swallows flew low in chase.

The Secret Dancer

The child was at that stage of awareness, of slowing its previous clumsiness down to an almost delicate precision. For those without patience, one more irritation.

The girl employed to look after her wholly delighted in her, such a child was a new experience. And the child's mother was rarely at home to be exasperated by the hours her daughter spent at meals, walks, baths, bedtime. Isobel Anstruther was a businesswoman, with shops to run, and evenings up to her toque in entertainment. In the upper levels of her tall townhouse was a nursery section, bedroom for child, bedroom for the au pair, a play-cum-sittingroom with television, and a bathroom. The au pair was Irish, Jennifer Darcy, not come to learn English, but to take some GCE A-levels for university entrance.

At first sight she was a plain girl, but on closer examination was one of those who are like the Gothic shrouded chrysalis of the butterfly they will become, even hanging their hair as if it had been carved to fit a narrow case. Some of the reasons for the suppression of her animation could be that her parents, a Dublin lawyer and a frustrated cello-player forced to bring up children and run a home, had believed she should become a ballet dancer. For eight years she had lived like a nun whose daily penance was to twist and elevate her body to the command of a bronchial piano. She had passed all her grades with the detached accomplishment required of one dedicated to turning her life and body into an art form, her entrechats and pliés, her arabesques, all exquisite. Till it was discovered she had grown to five foot nine inches.

Her employer had used her father in the purchase and setting-up of a branch shop in Dublin. Thus the connection. There was little doubt that the girl was a pleasing person to have around. She moved lightly, unobtrusively, was attentive to the slightest word, spoke rarely, obeyed implicitly, at times almost like a saintly automaton. But sometimes laughter would descend the slenderly balustraded staircase to the fanlit hallway below. The child would have her in fits.

The child had been named Amanda because it rang well with her parents belief in their position in life, it fitted with their décor and their friends. It had no personal significance.

It had taken Amanda quite a while to accept the new overseer of her daily routine. But two factors had contributed. The first was that nobody before had ever paid her so much attention. The second was when she happened to wake one night, disturbed by sounds, and emerged onto the darkened landing. The door of the sitting-room was open. Music was playing, and she could not at first comprehend what she saw. A figure flew and twirled about the room. She clung to the doorpost, watching. It was as if Jennifer had turned into a fairytale creature, for the lightness and swiftness of her movement suggested something magical. And then the dancer noticed her, and without change of expression, pirouetted across and gathered her up, so that the child, too, felt light as magic as she was whirled about the room. The experience was so agreeable she began to giggle and then to laugh. Round and round the room they went. And then there was another figure in the doorway. A man in a dinner-jacket.

Henry Anstruther watched for a few moments before coughing to announce in tones he realised were preposterously pedantic, his presence and the lateness of the hour. As the girl apologised, all he was aware of was the heaving of her chest, pushing towards him a pair of pulmonary domes he had not noticed before.

The child did not resent being returned to her room, tucked up in bed, her mind still flew through the air. Her father descended to his drawing-room to pour out a cognac and dwell upon what he had witnessed. He, too, had been as amazed as his daughter. He decided not to tell his wife as she sat absorbed in the perusal of a report she needed for the morning. He felt slightly irritated by the artificial colouring of her hair, the myriad tints catching the light.

Jennifer had been mortified at his discovery of her dancing. It had been the music that had started her. Respighi's Birds. She had been only half aware of picking Amanda up, incorporating her into her thralldom to the music. Later, as she stripped and washed away the unaccustomed sweat from her body, she remembered the intensity of Henry Anstruther's eyes dwelling on her as she apologised.

In the morning the round and lustrous eyes of her charge saw her with favoured accord. It was not that they pursued her with dogged devotion from then on. It was simply that the child had a great deal to say, and at last felt she had found someone she could talk to. And

Jennifer always listened, often could not help laughing at the child's preponderous statements.

The weeks then passed, she and the child in an absorbed relationship, the household downstairs a distant hum of high-powered social and business boilerhouse.

One night when she returned late from her evening classes and thought the house retired to bed early, for at first impression all was dark and silent, something unexpected happened.

She had gone into the kitchen first to make a cup of coffee. She washed up the cup afterwards, turned out the lights and passed into the hall. Suddenly a burst of conversation erupted from the drawing-room, and she glanced in surprise into a room . . . that she did not recognise. It was filled with people in fancy-dress, splendid long silk gowns, braided velvet coats, powdered wigs. The room itself was full of gilt-framed mirrors, rich brocade curtains, a great glass chandelier. She blinked as if to clear and sharpen her vision, and the movement of her eyelids was like a switch, turning it off. She blinked again as if expecting it to turn on again, kept blinking. But there was nothing. Only darkness. She reached inside the doorway and switched on the lights.

Spotlamps and great mushroom tablelamps threw the empty room alight. There was the huge purple Craigie Aitchison taking up one wall, the centre of the room filled with the square leather couches, the Giacometti stood in its corner beside the small Bridget Riley she liked, the green Francis Bacon she hated was over the mantelpiece. Her skin prickling a little, she entered the room. She crossed over to the television. Its screen was like a dish of polished granite, cold to the touch. She was tempted to turn it on, as if it might have been responsible, as if television sets might secretly indulge themselves after their owners had retired to bed. She checked the battery of aluminium-faced stereo and video equipment, touched the knobs and dials. But it too was cold and dead, all its little lights dark.

By the next morning she had forgotten all about it. She had to take Amanda to the dentist. The Anstruthers appeared to refer from time to time to some instruction manual on the care of children, and Jennifer would take their daughter for checks on her eyes, teeth, deportment, mind and general health to a variety of opulent consultants.

If the day were fine she would stop the taxi home on the far side of the park, so that they could walk back at leisure, throw crisps to the Mandarin ducks, have a go on the swings, a spin on the roundabout, play hide-and-seek among the trees. Amanda was an earnest player of this game and for one so young could hide so thoroughly it sometimes took Jennifer ten minutes and rising anxiety to find her. Once she hid inside the metal pram-barrow used by a park-keeper and was wheeled away without making a sound, much to the man's astonishment when he tipped her onto the compost heap.

This day Amanda had read a sign that said No Dogs, and agreed that it spoke truly because there weren't any. When told its real meaning, she insisted they play at being dogs, till Jennifer was embarrassed at being found barking on all fours by a pair of prim uniformed nannies wheeling their prams among the trees.

That evening there was a dinner-party downstairs, the meal organised by caterers. Bursts of laughter would rise up through the house, shaking it like gusts of wind. Jennifer was listening to folk-songs on the radio as she wrote a letter to her mother when suddenly the door of the sitting-room swung wide, and there was a pause, as if there was about to be the advent of something large such as a wheelchair. She got up not knowing quite what to expect. Standing in the doorway were Henry Anstruther and another man, both in shirt-sleeves and ties, and holding onto each other. They were looking at her as people stand and regard creatures in their zoo cages.

—Sorry to intrude, my dear, said Henry Anstruther, his speech slurred. We hoped we might find you at your nocturnal activities.

She blushed scarlet when she realised what he was referring to. It was obvious they were both very drunk. She had not noticed before that he had a small pot-belly. Both men had them, so that they stood there like Teniel's Tweedle Dee and Tweedle Dum. But despite his befuddlement, Henry Anstruther had realised how clumsy the scene was. He reached to close the door.

—Very sorry, my dear. Please forgive us. He had half-closed the door, when he swung it back again.

—This is Mortimer, he introduced his companion, beginning to close the door again. Known to his friends as Mort. Or even Death. The last words said after the door had shut. She heard them laughing at the joke as they went downstairs.

At breakfast in the kitchen he was extremely contrite, though some of that could have been put down to his feeling rather ill. His apologies between gulps of black coffee were so drawn out that, with Amanda interrupting to try and tell of the dream she had had and Isobel Anstruther bustling in with handfuls of lists, telling him he'd be late at his office, he forgot what he was saying most of the time.

They spent much of that day in the park, fed half a stale loaf to the swans and ducks, then met two small friends and there was much chasing and playing about, so that Jennifer was able to sit on a bench and give one eye to research on the Brontes, Bramwell's influence on his sisters in particular. As the lunch-hour drew near, the children's games became more fractious and ended in tears. Amanda returned, her skirt covered in grass stains, mud on her face and knees.

—An early scrub for you tonight, young lady, said Jennifer, as they returned home.

In common with most children, Amanda's baths were not, as far as she was concerned, anything to do with washing. They were occasions for indulging in the whole spirit of water. Jenifer, leaning over the edge to dive in with assaults of soap, became soaked, and decided that night it might be easier to take her clothes off and get in with her. Amanda, who had been blowing bubbles, started to laugh with near hysterical happiness, the water now risen up to her armpits and the soft slippery limbs of Jennifer all around her. And while she enjoyed these new sensations, in no time at all Jennifer had managed to wash her from head to foot. Amanda slid about like a small pink fish.

—You make the water so deep, she crooned. I'd like it always like this.

When he opened the door, Henry Anstruther was anticipating the scene he usually found when he entered on his daughter's bathnight. For a moment his vision was confused by the comparative emptiness of the bathroom and the fullness of the bath. His opened mouth finally focused, as did his eyes, upon the pink spheres of Jennifer's breasts rising from the water.

—It's lovely, Daddy, crowed Amanda. You come in too. We can make room. Then the water will be really deep.

But he had already retreated, swinging the door after him with a muttered apology.

—Why didn't Daddy want to come in with us? questioned the child, as Jennifer, a towel over her own shoulders, rubbed her over-vigorously with another in her embarrassment.

—We'd have been a terrible squash, she replied.

—I should have loved it, sighed the child, squirming from the abrasion of the towel.

Henry Anstruther returned later to say goodnight to his daughter. Jennifer heard the small piping voice demanding to know where her mother was, and being reminded she was in Manchester and wouldn't be back till late that night. She knew he would knock on her door and busied herself tidying up Amanda's toys. She was standing with an armful of crayons and papers as he entered.

—I seem to have blundered in on you rather a lot lately, he apologised.

She was thrown into further confusion by the way he looked at her.

—Come down and have a drink, he suggested. Perhaps you'd like to play something on the stereo. There's no point in you sitting cooped up here.

—Thank you, she replied, feeling it would be impolite to refuse. Would it be all right after I come back from my class?

When she came downstairs later that night, after returning from her lecture, she was mostly nervous of being alone with him, so that her mind was totally unprepared for what happened as she turned into the drawing-room.

It seemed to burst upon her, the clamour of voices, the crowd of people in the room, the flickering sharpness of so many points of yellow-gold candlelight, a strange sticky smell, all the faces turning towards her. She saw much more this time, the knee breeches of the men, their buckled shoes, the puff sleeves of their long dresses, their glittering jewellery, the high colour of their faces. The buzz of conversation diminished because they seemed to be equally disconcerted by her appearance, everyone staring at her. She found she could neither move nor speak. Behind her she felt a cold blast of air as if the front door were open. She felt her eyes closing, as if to suppress some sort of pain in her body.

When she opened them again, to save herself from falling, she found she was looking across the familiar Anstruther drawing-room, straight at Henry, standing alone beside the stereo.

—Are you all right? he asked, coming across the room quickly. She was holding onto the doorpost, and he took her by the arm and led her to a chair.

—I'll fix you a drink. Brandy, I should think. The liquid was fiery in her throat.

—I just came over faint, she said, not seeing how she could explain it any other way. He might think her touched if she told him what she had seen, especially after everything else.

—Better now? he asked.

She nodded, pushing herself back in the chair to conceal a shiver. He stood looking down at her, his head on one side.

—I'll bet you haven't had any supper. Aren't I right?

She shrugged.

—I never eat much anyway.

—Come on, he insisted, pulling her to her feet. I haven't had anything myself tonight.

In the kitchen she set about making two omelettes while he cut bread and opened a bottle of wine. She found her movements stiff, beating the eggs, lifting the iron pan. She felt she had been physically shocked by what she had seen, as well as frightened. But the effects of the brandy, the smell of melting butter, and the light-hearted banter of Henry Anstruther in the domestic atmosphere of the kitchen, all combined to restore her.

—You young girls are all the same, never eating, always worrying about your figure.

—I don't really worry about it, you know, she said gravely. I forget. Or I just don't feel hungry. Sometimes I'm like a little dog, I lick up Amanda's scraps. I hate to see good food wasted.

This was the longest speech Henry Anstruther had heard her make, and he smiled at her with pleasure. He was not a man intentionally setting out to seduce a young girl, though he could not have denied that the thought had crossed his mind. What he wanted to do was to make her dance again. He did not ply her with too much wine, but encouraged her to open out, to talk about her family. He told her stories about his own.

—My grandfather collected carpets. He had a big rambling house in the country, with plenty of rooms, but with as little furniture in them as possible so one could see the carpets. People used to call the house the Mosque. He built fountains in the garden, hoping it might persuade people to call it the Alhambra instead, which would have been worse, that being the name of the fleapit in the town. There were carpets on the walls, and in some rooms they were ten thick on the floor. His biggest enemy in life was moths. Constant wars with flit guns and sprays. And we came near to breaking our necks on mothballs.

She laughed. They took the remainder of their wine into the drawing-room.

—What sort of music do you like? he asked.

—I don't mind, she replied.

He thought he knew exactly what she would respond to, but that it could all come to nothing if he were too obvious. He put on a disco number by Donna Summer.

—Shake up my supper, he said.

He pushed the coffee-table out of the way and began to jig about in time to the beat, as the speakers poured the harsh driving music into the room.

—Come on, he invited, careful not to look at her, rolling his head, his eyes closed.

She had no suspicion of his motives. The rhythm was compulsive, urged her to move. The wine in her blood helped release her restraint.

Christ, he thought. How the little Gothic maiden can move. He smiled at her as they danced, trying to make his gaze seem casual. Music seemed to transform her, bring her to life. After three tracks he was exhausted, quietly changed the record for Vivaldi's *Four Seasons*, his hand shaking, afraid she might wonder at the arbitrary contrast, that it was the wrong choice. But he knew, as soon as the music swept out of the speakers, swirled round the room, drowning its furnishings, that she would respond.

After pushing back the sofas, he splashed brandy over his fingers, unable to take his eyes from her, his hand still shaking, but now from nervous excitement. He wondered if he was just ignorant of the act of dancing, of performers, prejudiced because he had always thought of her before as no more than a mouse. Bodies in his experience were heavy objects, clumsy to move quickly, difficult to lift far off the ground. Yet she seemed to shed all weight, rose without effort like a windblown leaf. It was an extension of human activity he had never in his life observed at close quarters. Perhaps he was a little drunk. Perhaps he was imagining more to it than there was. At times it seemed the music blew her about the room; at other times he heard nothing, was only aware of this acrobatic human dragonfly, who rose as high as the ceiling, crossed the room with the speed of a skater, spun as if on a coin, then in slow motion hypnotised him with her sinuous control.

Jennifer knew she was showing off, but she didn't care, she wanted to let herself go. She saw Henry standing by the stereo, glass in hand, smiling in admiration, thought she smiled back at him but was too lost to the music to be certain. The power within her body was pure joy to her.

Henry Anstruther suddenly felt he wanted to put out a hand, stop her, enfold her in his arms, tell her she was magical, would she dance for him every night of his life.

—Christ, said Isobel Anstruther, standing in the doorway.

Nodody had heard her enter the house. But her expletive broke the spell. Jennifer came back to earth, one foot hit the carpet like a hammer, and she stood swaying, a taut bundle of sweat-soaked sinews, her lungs pumping rasps of air in and out. Henry stood drained of all reaction save guilt for his last thought.

—I wouldn't have believed it of you, Jennifer, Isobel Anstruther said, shaking her head. Only I see you there now. I had no idea you could do that sort of thing.

Her voice had already begun to change from admiration to sarcasm as she read her husband's face.

—I'm sorry, cried Jennifer, and she ran from the room, pulling her exhausted sweat-soaked body up the stairs. In her room, she threw herself upon her bed, and lay like a log, completely spent.

—What a shame about your height, Isobel Anstruther said to her, next morning down in the kitchen. But I would have thought you would still make a marvellous dancer. I'd no idea you were so talented.

Jennifer shook her head, smiling nervously.

—I hope you didn't mind, she said, about last night.

Isobel Anstruther was not her usual rushing self. She put an arm round the girl's shoulder.

—Why should I mind? Wish I'd seen all of it. Henry told me it was unbelievable.

Amanda had overheard and, after her mother had left, asked Jennifer why she hadn't danced with her again. She promised she would.

It so happened that when they were in the park that day, there came the sound of music in the distance. A lunchtime concert in the bandstand. When they were about fifty yards away, passing through a grove of oaks, Amanda stopped.

—Now we can dance, she said.

Jennifer had forgotten her promise and laughed.

Something about being lifted up high and swung about always seems to make small children squeal and laugh, and Amanda's joy made Jennifer laugh as well, so their dancing was a comic twirling round the treetrunks, the child trying to copy some of the girl's steps, her laughter rising into song whenever she was lifted high, instinctively stretching out her arms and legs in stubby arabesques. But however light the child, lifting her up and down soon exhausted Jennifer and she lay panting on the ground, while Amanda still danced in and out of the treetrunks.

She did not see Henry Anstruther that day and felt relieved. She felt partly ashamed, as if she had revealed to him a weakness, and partly afraid, as if desporting so before him might have given him power over her.

In the evening Isobel Anstruther told her that Henry and she were going down to spend the weekend with her mother, taking Amanda with them, so she would be left on her own, could do what she liked. They would be back on Sunday afternoon. Jennifer thought it odd that the highly organised Isobel hadn't mentioned it before.

The next day at breakfast Henry Anstruther kept looking at her, as if he wished to say something to her. But his wife kept charging in and out of the kitchen with the manic unexpectedness of a chinchilla so that he never managed it; and soon, Jennifer, afraid of his glances, took Amanda upstairs.

Isobel was back in the early afternoon, the car was packed, and they set off just ahead of the rush-hour. And Jennifer was left in the empty, silent house.

Outside, traffic, people, noises, never ceased. But within the house there was a hollow of peace, an architectural cavern, a furnished tower, her own room level with the tops of trees in the street. She revised some lecture notes on George Eliot, then wrote an essay. When it began to grow dark she went down to the kitchen and ate a slice of quiche, gave the chronically somnolent cat a saucer of tinned meat, then went out, caught a bus. From a call-box she rang the number of a girl she knew from the tech. But she was out, so she went to a cinema on her own.

The film keyed her up to a high pitch of emotional intensity. All the way back to the house she was entirely wrapped up with reflections. The girl had been her own age. Violette Nozerre.

But the moment she entered the house, turned on the hall lights, she forgot the film. A cold fear gripped her. The door of the drawing-room was open. Inside was darkness, a waiting stillness. She wanted to run past it, rush up the stairs. But instead, as if hypnotised by her own fear, she could not stop staring at it, her hackles stiff. With intense compulsion she began to walk towards it, anticipating that at any moment something would happen. A grandfather clock ticked, her skirt rustled, floorboards beneath the carpet gave muffled creaks. She stretched out a hand to hold onto the architrave. There was not the slightest hint of anything about to happen, save the pounding of her senses.

She slid a hand round to find the light switches, fingers almost frantic to plunge them downwards, afraid they might fail.

The spotlamps and mushroom globes sprang into quiet illumination, the room spread before her, at rest. Her heart beat loudly. She entered slowly, found she was still holding her breath and let it out painfully, stood breathing hard. She switched on the television and on the instant an interviewer appeared to underline with loud emphasis, the present and its monetary obsessions. She sat down and gradually calm returned to her.

She worked on her books all the next morning. Only when seated at the small table in the kitchen alcove at lunchtime, drinking a cup of coffee, did she think of Henry Anstruther again. She thought that she had never seen him show the slightest sign of affection for his wife. They behaved more like two people who work in the same office. She had seen Isobel kiss him with the same precision that she licked the flap of an envelope. The only time they smiled unwittingly was at their daughter, the small emotive go-between. She missed Amanda, despite not having to worry what she was up to, the constant answering of questions, having to amuse her. She had grown fond of her. She did like Henry Anstruther, she thought. It was pleasant to be in his company. If only he had never seen her dance, never caught her in the bath with Amanda, never entered the secret gates of her private domain.

During the afternoon she did some exercises. She did a few every day, partly out of habit, partly from the pleasure of keeping supple. That night she decided she would go down and listen to music on the stereo. She did not actually think, in so many words, that she might feel inclined to dance, but knew with clandestine excitement that she would. Just in case, she put on her dancing slippers. Among the records she found a copy of *Petrushka*. She had taken part in a school version, had actually performed the name part, there being no boys at the school. The electrifying first bars were enough. She ran round pushing the sofas back, and she was off, the music like a great hand lifting her, sweeping her about the room. Where she forgot she improvised, danced the other parts, the Moor and the Doll. By the time she was the ghost of Petrushka, her body was wringing with sweat. As the music ended, she sank into a sofa.

The ensuing silence began to weigh emptily. She got up to put on more music. Something quiet, meditative. She found a Bach fugue, and began to dance slowly and reflectively, in a series of textbook movements.

There was no exact moment of change. She could not have said what her vision saw one second before. But now, with eye-polished intensity, she saw only that the room was suddenly full of people. They were all around her, but moving back. The detail of their eighteenth-century costumes was overpoweringly real. The din of the chattering diminished as they stared at her in horror. There was whispering, a woman with a fan was addressing her. But she felt herself gripped by some sort of pain, a paralysis that kept her limbs rigid. Sounds were stuck in her throat, her hearing seemed to be clogging, her vision fading. Her last sight was reflected from mirror to mirror, over everyone's heads; the great globe of candle flames and glass droplets of the chandelier. Then she fell forwards onto waxed floorboards, heard fading gasps and screams around her, then heard no more.

Consciousness returned as if it had been a long time absent. She became aware of a pulsating beat, something like a mower outside cutting the lawn. There was a strange face a few feet away. Her moment of alarm faded as she saw it was the somnolent cat crouched near her, contentedly purring. She raised her head. She found herself lying on the soft carpeted floor of the drawing-room. Full daylight was streaming in. She sat up, her body stiff and cold. The stereo was humming, the lights were still on. She got up and turned them off. She could hear pigeons cooing on the eaves. She sat down on a sofa and tried to think.

The cat was sitting upright before her, still purring, opening its green half-closed eyes every now and then to regard her with a sort of anticipatory pleasure. She knew what it wanted, and bent down to stroke its soft neck, pleased by the reassurance of its normality. Then she got up to go into the kitchen.

Halfway across the hall the eager cat got between her legs and tripped her up. She avoided falling but crashed against the hall table. As she set everything back in place, she found herself face to face with a framed page from an old journal. She had often meant to read it. It was supposed to describe something that had happened in this very house over 150 years ago.

A Double Tragedy. During the pleasantries of an autumn soirée held at No. 18 Crundall Place, the town residence of Mr and Mrs George Darling, upon the evening of the fifth of September, 1805, the guests were struck with amazement and horror when a fashionably-dressed lady wearing a theatre cloak rushed into their midst and fell dead at their feet, a pair of sewing shears protruding from her back. Moments later an hysterical maidservant tumbled downstairs to announce that Mrs. Darling lay poisoned on her bedroom floor. Mr Darling was immediately overcome and had to be assisted into his library. An investigation had brought to light the explanation for this tragic misfortune. The lady stabbed was a Miss Grace Cunningham, a dancer from the Hippodrome and particular friend of Mr Darling. It seems that when Miss Cunningham arrived at the house, Mrs Darling tried to push her out, and when she resisted, took up a pair of scissors and thrust them into her. Thereupon in a fit of remorse at her terrible deed, she rushed upstairs and partook of an entire bottle of laudanum, with the result that she presently expired. We offer our deepest sympathies to Mr Darling, who is now left with neither lady to console him.

Jennifer reread it a second time while the somnolent cat twined itself gently round her legs. In some agitation she went into the kitchen and switched on the kettle for coffee while she fed the animal. She made some toast and sat on a stool to eat it. On the terracotta tiles of the floor a pattern of leaf shadows danced and writhed round the cat as it contentedly cleaned its whiskers. She washed up her mug and plate quickly, tidied everything away and went upstairs.

She ran a bath. While lying in the warm clear water her anxiety began to diminish. She thought back on what had happened in the drawing-room the night before. It seemed now no more than a dream, a nightmare. But even so she considered the packing of her suitcase, remembering that she must collect unironed clothes from downstairs, the writing of a letter to Isobel Anstruther, and telephoning her friend from the tech. to ask if her mother would put her up for the night while she looked for a room.

Later, she dried her hair, then lay back on the pillows and reflected that it was not necessarily a warning that one should run away from. It was just a warning. She stared through the window at the green leaves dancing on their branches like small creatures restrained by leashes, restless children gripped by their parents. She heard in her mind Amanda's laughter, her small voice enunciating words with slow curving precision.

While the Country Sleeps

By midnight the great terminus was almost deserted. Without throngs of people it seemed far dirtier. All the shops were shuttered, the offices darkened. Hollow sounds echoed back from the cathedral-high roof, the odd voice, the sudden burst of a diesel's exhaust as it put muscle into heaving away a line of coaches until morning, or a sudden flapping of pigeons' wings as a group cascaded upwards, seemingly uninterested in sleep. A few people sprawled on benches. A small queue waited outside a mobile canteen. There was a ripple of laughter as a boy at the counter ordered twenty-two coffees, eleven cokes, three teas and an orangeade. Occasionally someone would appear, hurrying across to the yawning official at the barrier of Platform 13 to ask the time of the last train. Each time the official would turn as if to point to the information board, before remembering it was blank, then tell him he had half an hour to wait. There were a few trains lying at platforms. But they were darkened and silent, part of the station furniture.

A man sat on one of the long benches, an open paperback in one hand. His fingers sank into the soft sides of the cup of coffee he had purchased and he had to put it down swiftly, having forgotten that the only way to avoid burning one's fingers was to lift the cup by the rim. He would read a few sentences, take a sip of coffee, draw on his cigar, then look round to glance at a distant clock, or regard some late-comer wandering about impatiently, or tilt his head back to watch a flock of pigeons sweep beneath the girders of the vast barrel roof as freely as if they were flying between trees in the open countryside. He enjoyed savouring a book when reading, hated hurrying through the chapters as if the only purpose were to discover the conclusion. Besides, the journey he waited to commence was a long one.

Quite soon, the flat yellow face of a diesel slid slowly up to the buffers of Platform 13. Its approach from behind rows of parked baggage trolleys, railings and information boards was heralded by a vibration that one sensed rather than heard before it actually appeared.

He selected a corner seat and hoisted his case up onto the rack. There was not more than a dozen people in the entire carriage, their faces shut up within themselves, as they settled down, full of their private thoughts, much as he must have appeared himself, the man supposed. The expression of a young woman a few seats down, whose clothes and shoulder-bag matched each other like the textures of a burnt winter landscape, suggested to him defensiveness, a fear of being stormed. Maybe behind the mask she was not like that at all. She didn't even bother to look round her.

For a while he lapsed into his book. But the lights in the waiting carriage were dim, and his mind wandered. He could hear a number of noisy youths chatting behind him. He thought they sounded a little drunk. They were talking of a football match they had been to. Diagonally across the carriage behind the glass screen that cut off the central outer door, he could see a blond woman leaning out of the window, talking to a man down on the platform. There was a kind of settled air about everyone. He remembered as a student rushing to catch the last train many times, usually with a girl who lived in Chelmsford. They were invariably late, out of breath, giggling, and there were always others who just made it, so that the carriage as the train pulled out was filled with panting laughter and breathless bursts of conversation. They would settle to earnest or cynical discussion of the film they had just seen, everyone around them talking, laughing, animating the midnight train. But the atmosphere in this train seemed one of empty resignation.

A guard walked past the windows backwards, waving an arm, and seconds later, with an imperceptible shiver, the train was gliding along the platform, picking up speed. The blond woman pulled up the window and came to sit down in the seats across the gangway. She was wearing a scarlet Russian shirt belted at the waist. She smiled at him as she sat down. The man watched her over the pages of his book. She still smiled, though looking down at the table in reflection. There was a lustre in her eyes. Must be from whomever she had bidden goodbye, he thought. If one were to try drawing her, she would seem not unlike Punch in a blond wig, long protruding jaw, hooked nose. Yet the overall impression was of an attractive person, liveliness and colour that refreshed her features. Her eyelashes were blond, so the thick masses of golden curls must have been real.

His interest, always little more than a cameo-painter's, returned to his book. He was already slightly irritated that the peace of the carriage was being eroded by the youths, who were free-ranging from one group of empty seats to another, rowdy in the security of their numbers, making provocatively uncouth remarks to each other for the benefit of other passengers, as they wandered up and down. They seemed particularly concerned with the smells of private parts of their anatomies.

The train had passed through the dark groins of brickwork of the station approaches, where the occasional lamp emphasised its gloomy appearance as if they were travelling through some vast crypt, and was now among dimmed, shadowy office blocks and canyons of old brick houses, slipping through ghostly suburban stations.

He looked up, aware the woman was talking, that she might be addressing him since there was no one else seated there. But she was looking down the passageway, replying to something one of the youths had said from behind him. She was smiling, speaking cheerfully. Maybe her appearance was a bit tarty, the man thought, surprised by the ease with which she seemed to have leapt into conversation. Her voice was fluid and pleasant.

Suddenly one of the youths appeared and, with the indolent ease of a cat, slipped into the seat opposite her. Another followed and draped himself over the headrest of the seat beside her. The man caught her glance and saw the faintest glimmer of alarm there. But she smiled amicably at him. Her own fault, he thought. She practically invited them.

—Been on a visit then? the first one asked. He was thin-faced, short-haired, quite good-looking. He was aggressive as if unsure of himself.

—I came up to see an exhibition, she replied, easily.

—At Olympia? asked the other, round-faced, with a bush of curly hair. His voice was nonchalant, cynical.

She shook her head.

—Paintings, she replied. At the Tate gallery. Have you ever been there?

Liar, the man thought with amusement. He knew the Tate was closed that day. That man she had been so dewy-eyed over was her lover. She was exercising the lies she was taking home to tell her husband.

—I wouldn't waste my time, replied the round-faced boy rudely.

The man wondered what he would do if they started to insult her. Should he order them to leave her alone, pretending some kind of authority? Suppose they attacked him? He glanced upwards to see how far he was from the communication cord. He knew that he did not possess a cool head in moments of stress.

—Isn't that the place that paid thousands of quid for a pile of bricks? asked the short-haired boy. Bloody stupid, if you ask me. Did you see them?

She nodded.

—You're right. I think it's a load of rubbish. But there are some beautiful paintings there. By Picasso and Matisse, Renoir, Cézanne and lots of Turners. Do you like paintings?

The short-haired youth seemed taken aback, as if he had not expected the conversation to take this line.

—I was quite good at technical drawing, he replied.

Another youth had stopped to join them, his back to the man, so that the woman seemed even more hemmed in.

—The art teacher's a fairy, he said. All we do is piss about.

—Are you still at school? she asked.

The man caught her eye again, saw that she was assessing him for reassurance, that he at least was there, should she need rescuing. Her smile was very warm, he thought.

—One more term, replied the short-haired youth.

—I expect you're glad to be leaving, she said. Will it be difficult finding a job when you leave?

—In Colchester it will. There's loads of unemployment.

—What sort of industry have you got?

Quite quickly a discussion grew, the youths seeming eager on finding someone sympathetic, rushing like thirsty creatures to the water's edge. Their intimidating attitudes vanished, the air was clear of threat.

—Even without a job, it's better than being at school, said the short-haired boy, leaning his elbows on the table. I mean, we get money. Don't have to get it off our parents.

—They don't care at school, said the round-faced boy. It's just filling in time. Anybody'd get bored.

—I know , she agreed. They concentrate all their efforts on those taking O-levels, and don't bother with the rest.

She was smiling attentively at them and let a smile slip through to the man just to show she was managing. She was charming them, he thought. With great skill. Taming them, drawing them out to talk about themselves. Almost a professional job. He wondered what she was.

He glanced out of the window. Lamplit streets passed by like trills of piano-played light. Then rows of houses like grey envelopes with orange postage stamps. They were still passing through the city outskirts. Surprising how many people were still awake in their bedrooms.

There was a slight lull in the chatter, and he heard one of the youths ask what she did.

—I'm a school-teacher, she replied, and laughed at their expressions.

—Never, exclaimed the short-haired youth. Are you kidding?

—I teach Art and P.E. at the Comprehensive.

—Are you married then? asked the round-faced boy.

—I'm divorced, she replied.

—Suddenly the questions became personal; the intimidating air had returned, as if it seized upon the sexuality of such revelations. The man held onto his book stiffly, listening.

—D'you have a boyfriend? asked the short-haired youth. You must have. I bet you have. And he laughed coarsely.

—Teachers have loads of holidays, don't they? asked the boy who was standing. I'll bet you get around.

—Sleep around, too, I'll be bound, said the round-faced youth. With any of the boys you teach?

The woman never lost her poise, just a quick smile passed through the blockade of male arms and hips to the man who blinked back a vague morse-code of reassurance.

—I have a daughter of nineteen, she replied. She's at teacher-training college. I live a very normal life.

—So many surprises, said the short-haired boy. You don't look old enough, really, you don't.

—If all teachers were like you, school'd be all right, grumbled the round-faced boy.

—But it's easy talking to three of you. When there's a class of thirty, all wanting something different, all hating school, it can be difficult. And some of you like giving us a hard time. I'll bet you've got trouble-makers in your class, haven't you?

—Maybe, agreed the short-haired boy. But why don't they make the classes more interesting? They always stick to the same old boring routines.

—All right, she agreed. Tell me what sort of subjects you'd like to do?

Once more the atmosphere of threat melted away. The man sighed and relaxed, slipped back into his book. There were long stretches of dark emptiness outside now, countryside black and shapeless in the night. Then suddenly they were back into a lacework of streetlamps, silhouettes of terraced housing, brightly illuminated factories, the train's brakes grinding.

—This is me, said the woman, gathering her bag. Thank you for making the journey go so pleasantly, and I wish you all success in finding jobs after you leave school.

The youths seemed abashed as she rose, stepping back before her as if in gaining her height she had assumed the proportions of the school-teacher she had said she was. As the train drew into the station, she bid each of them goodbye, with her cheerful, easy smile, her eyes glowing. And she turned to nod a smile of goodbye to the man. He nodded a fleeting quiver of the lips in return. They all watched her alight. As her head passed by the window she looked in and smiled again. The man felt he should have risen and bowed in acknowledgement of her performance.

Perhaps he had imagined it all, he thought, as the train waited, doors slamming, passengers passing, a trolley-load of sacks trundling in the opposite direction. Maybe there had been no threat at all. They were no more than bored lads who had struck up a conversation with a friendly woman. As the train set off into the night again, they were talking amongst themselves.

—Why'd you lot have to butt in? the short-haired youth was complaining. I had her eating out of my hand. If you hadn't been there, I could have had her knickers off, you could see she was a right sort.

—Yeah, and cows can fly, jeered one of the others.

They argued for a while, then split up, ranging up and down the carriage again. Most of the seats were empty now, and they sat about at random, never remaining anywhere for long.

The man sank back into his book. It was a good book and it absorbed him each time he returned to it. But the restlessness of the youths was like a draught, not actually disturbing, but a nagging disquiet. They seemed curiously volatile, unstable.

He became aware later of a girl's voice in amongst their conversation and adjusted his seat slightly so as not to appear inquisitive but to allow him to see down the central aisle. They were perched like a flock of birds about a group of seats at the far end of the carriage. He could see the top half of a girl's face. She looked and sounded young, not much older than they. He could not make out what they were saying, but though the interchange sounded reasonable, he could tell there was a certain strain in the girl's voice. Being young, she was more vulnerable than the woman-teacher, the man thought. Yet she too was talking well, creating conversation. Not quite as if her life depended on it, but with a certain amount of detectable anxiety. If they started anything rough with her, he would simply pull the cord, he thought. One scream or cry, just one.

He sat back, and returned to his book, one ear cocked. The printed words before him changed into the near reality of people, living in a city strange to him, and their voices filled his head; till the grinding of the train's brakes intruded, and he looked out at the sleeping suburbs of Colchester. He had forgotten all about the youths. They were gathering their anoraks, the girl was lifting her case down, and they were still talking as he had last heard them. The reasonable chatter of old friends, he thought. They left the train together, passed his window in a group.

Would she get home safely? he wondered. Had he imagined the threat? Were they not just ordinary boys, bored, chatting up the birds? But his imagination fed on all the alternatives. Circumstances or personalities, just fractionally different, could have sent events off out of anybody's hands. And he still wondered how he would have reacted himself had anything happened. He was the one outsider aware, able to exercise a restraint. Perhaps his presence had done so all along.

He was alone in the carriage now. Outside, the passing of the black sleeping countryside was marked only by the slow traverse of an occasional point of light. He was barely a quarter through his book when the train drew into its destination, Ipswich. There were about a dozen people left to alight. The man transferred to his connection, a small dimly-lit train waiting the other side of the platform. Its old-fashioned carriages had compartments and a side passage. Apart from one compartment in which four railwaymen were playing cards, it appeared to be empty.

He selected a compartment at random. The underfloor engine ticked over quietly at the far end of the carriage. It was half past two in the middle of the night. He could look across a number of platforms towards the lighted windows of an office beneath the signals box, where the silhouettes of a number of men moved about as if each were rehearsing to himself the lines of a speech. The big blue whale of a locomotive slid past the office, drawing a number of darkened carriages, passing behind another diesel waiting by itself, its driver leaning out of his cab, hands folded round each other. Much activity in the middle of the night, the man thought. Except in his train. But after half-an-hour it pulled out.

When he went down the passageway to the lavatory, even the

compartment that had contained the cardplayers was empty. Nobody came to check his ticket. The train rattled through the night, lacking the swift smoothness of the previous train. The blackness outside was like an endless tunnel. When the train drew into his station, he was the only person to alight. He shut the door with a solitary bang. There was nobody on the platform. No head looked out. Almost immediately the train drew out, seemingly of its own accord. It could have been a ghost train. The slightly misty night-sky rose above him like a huge vault.

He crossed over the footbridge. There were a few single bulbs burning in the station. But it was completely deserted. He crossed the cinders to the carpark in the coalyard to unlock his car.

It was a loneliness he could almost revel in. The woman with whose mind and body he had spent the last two days and nights would be fast asleep now, he thought. With the rest of the country. Her mind in dreams and her body as peaceful as the dark fields all around.